PUFFIN BOOKS
Editor : Kaye Webb

The Moon in the Cloud

At a time extremely long ago, the very time as it happened
when the Lord God stirred and grumbled, 'They're all bad down
there, except the Noahs, I'll have a flood,' there was one other
good and deserving couple in Israel : Reuben and Thamar.
Even Noah, devoted as he was to the will of the Lord, worried
about them. He couldn't help thinking it a little unfair that
Ham, his own wayward and selfish son, should be set above
this gentle pair. Ham, of course, thought it only right and
proper. Just as he thought it entirely suitable that Reuben
should go off on the dangerous journey to Kemi in search of
cats and lions. He *said* he could get both Reuben and Thamar
on to the Ark, when the time came. But it wasn't his job to book
places on the Ark – and he forgot, as Noah never did, that the
Lord God was a watchful God.

*' Sometimes a book appears of such individuality that it
strikes one with a shock, as if there were suddenly a new note
in the musical scale. We call it originality . . . the tale is told
with humorous assurance, wit and charm, in sparkling
narrative : the beast-fable element – for all these animals show
distinguishable animal-hood, according to their kind – is
blended perfectly with the Old Testament simplicity which
describes the Lord God's grumbles, as well as his instructions
to faithful Noah.'* The Times Literary Supplement.

This book was awarded
Medal for an outstandin

D1351034

Rosemary Harris

The Moon in the Cloud

Puffin Books
in association with Faber & Faber

Puffin Books,
Penguin Books Ltd,
Harmondsworth, Middlesex, England
Penguin Books,
625 Madison Avenue, New York, New York 10022, U.S.A.
Penguin Books Australia Ltd,
Ringwood, Victoria, Australia
Penguin Books Canada Ltd,
2801 John Street, Markham, Ontario L3R 1B4, Canada
Penguin Books (N.Z.) Ltd,
182–190 Wairau Road, Auckland 10, New Zealand

First published by Faber & Faber 1968

Published in Puffin Books 1977

Made and printed in Great Britain by
C. Nicholls & Company Ltd
Set in Linotype Pilgrim

Contents

Author's Note

Kemi, or the Black Land, was an ancient name for Egypt. The Flood being movable, so to speak, I've set these happenings at the time of the Egyptian Old Kingdom with a young (fictional) king of the VIth Dynasty on the throne. When he came to rule, the two kingdoms of Upper (South) and Lower (North) Egypt had been long united, with Mennofer, later called Memphis, as capital near the Delta of the Nile; and so my king would have worn the combined White and Red Crowns of Upper and Lower Egypt.

He wasn't then known as Pharaoh, but he had no lack of titles: Sovereign, Majesty, Son of Re, the Horus, Lord of the Two Lands, Lord of Diadems; and Beloved of Two Ladies (in real life he didn't keep to two). And his gods could have been counted in hundreds. He himself was a god-king, and a pyramid-builder, although the larger of those royal tombs were already some hundreds of years old.

I've tried to avoid slips in the background of this story, but if there are some I shall make the cowardly excuse that most writers on ancient Egypt blandly disagree on detail, right down to the spelling of names. It would have been very much easier to write in terms of a later Egyptian age, but that would have been a little like dressing up ancient Britons in the bombazine and bustles of Victoria's time.

Anyway, I should like to acknowledge a particular debt to Leonard Cottrell's *The Lost Pharaohs* and *Life Under* the *Pharaohs*, Dorothy Hales Gary's and Robert Payne's *Sun, Stones and Silence*, Cyril Aldred's *The Egyptians*, and Dr. Barbara Mertz's *Temples, Tombs and Hieroglyphs*, as well as to the late Oscar Hammerstein II, who inspired my High Priest of Sekhmet's much inferior Old Kingdom forerunner of 'Do-re-mi', which appears on page 93.

Reuben and Thamar

At a time extremely long ago, the very time as it happened when the Lord God stirred and grumbled, 'They're all bad down there, except the Noahs, I'll have a flood,' the very humble early ancestor of all circuses existed in the land now called Israel. There were no great sawdust rings, no tigers, performing seals or milk-white waltzing horses, but only a ragged tent pitched wherever one could be pitched, and a few half-starved animals who did their simple tricks willingly enough, because they loved their master, but slowly from lack of food.

These were two cream-coloured dromedaries, from the desert; a handful of donkeys with huge meek eyes and stubborn wills; an ape from Barbary, who often wondered as he popped his fleas just how he got there; some red-eyed dogs half-wild with hunger; five placid, silly goats; and two huge elephants from the unknown land which lay far to the South-west – a land the people of the North had never visited nor lifted up their eyes on, for their priestly rulers had strictly forbidden any such impudence from the very start.

So it was the elephants who had wandered innocently far North and North again, seeking for a country where no snakes fell down your neck when you were sleeping, and no spearsmen lay in wait under the wheeling stars. And one day they appeared on the horizon just as the tribesmen were sitting down to their humble midday meal of succulent baked kid and thin wine.

The terror there had been, the cries and lamentations, the windy talk of how the Lord had sent a visitation! (He had seemed a little withdrawn just lately, as if something had displeased him.) It was a mirage sort of day, when the sky was full of two of everything, and the sight of four enormous beasts (two of them upside down) slowly approaching from the South-west was awe-inspiring. Certainly an elephant upside down *is* awe-inspiring, even if your conscience is all right. The tribesmen's consciences were black as a coalminer's lungs.

The long and the short of it was that they rose as one man, struck their tents, and departed as fast as they could for another place – where they set up the stone images they had lately carved, and worshipped them, and begged to be protected from the Lord God's vengeance, as displayed in elephants. Which, it must be admitted, displeased the Lord God even further, and made him hum a little as he worked out his plans for a great, magnificent flood.

The tent of the animal-tamer Reuben, and of Thamar his wife, remained, however, where it was. For one thing Reuben had a sick donkey on his hands, too ill to be moved. Her poor white belly was dark with sweat, and her flanks heaved as she lay on the ground, now and then raising her head to swallow a little water. For another thing Reuben had lost patience with his tribe over the matter of the idols, and they disliked him for his independence. Their dislike had increased since the week before, when the finest young men of the tribe had come to him dressed in scarlet and gold, with jingling anklets, and had said:

'Reuben, you who are an artist when you're not performing with these smelly beasts of yours, carve us an idol from this piece of stone, so that we may worship it next feast day. Carve it deep and cruel and strong, that – when we daub it with blood – we may still see its face smiling in satisfaction at the sacrifice.'

But Reuben had answered firmly though politely that he would not.

And the next day they had come, and the next, and the next: begging, promising reward, threatening; until he lost his temper and told them what he thought of them, and where they could go to with their idols. So they had left him in great anger, swearing to ruin him: him and his mangy animals too.

Thamar shook with terror as she combed out a camel. She buried her face in its soft woolly ash-coloured fur, and wished Reuben would be more tactful, and less intrepid. Life was hard enough already, and food difficult to get, and if they were also to be ruined –

She felt the pulse of life throb deep beneath the great beast's hide under her cheek, and took heart.

'Reuben,' she said wistfully, 'would it have been so very bad to compromise a little? If you carved but didn't worship, would it matter?'

'It is forbidden,' said Reuben shortly, 'and you know it, Thamar.' He looked into her face, and his tone softened. 'Beloved,' he added, 'this morning I made you a new song.' From his pocket he drew out a reed pipe, and began to play. The notes mounted clear and thrilling as the notes of a bird into the still air. Thamar listened, smiling; but in her heart she was thinking that you cannot eat a song.

When the tribesmen rose and fled before the elephants, Reuben, hearing the hubbub, left his tent. Northwards he saw a cloud of dust departing, which hid the young men in gold and scarlet carrying their idols. And southwards he saw the elephants approaching, slow, patient and benign, and with their doubles upside down.

Reuben whistled. Then he threw back his head and laughed.

'Animals,' he said aloud wonderingly, 'animals. They've

run away from *animals*. Thamar –' he called, 'Thamar – come and see!'

Thamar come out of the tent and joined him. She saw the elephants, and put a hand to her enchanting mouth. 'Oh,' she said, 'what big, long noses. Worse than Uncle Zebedee's.'

'So the tribe will destroy my living, will they?' Reuben swept a hand towards the oncoming elephants, whose benign though sorely-tried natures were at once apparent to his animal-lover's eye. 'Behold the performing animal of all performing animals! O Thamar, blessed be the Lord God, who has shown us that today I did right as an artist, and has sent me this reward.' And he went forward, chirruping softly, to meet the elephants and bring them in. Much later in the day, as they tended the grateful beasts and watered them, Thamar looked out across the parched land, and made a small sound of surprise.

'Reuben! Whose are those sand-coloured tents, a distance away, almost invisible in this strong light? Who, besides ourselves, has stayed behind?'

'Noah.'

Reuben's voice was not encouraging. He couldn't get on with the venerable old man. He admired him, he liked him, *but* – Noah had a way of listening to a song and saying he supposed it was all right, but he himself, being a plain man, didn't understand it. Which would not have been so bad – except for the note of self-satisfaction in his voice, as if no fool could doubt it was superior to be plain and unmusical. And then Noah, who owned many animals, was kind and fed them well, and tended them when they were ill so that they prospered and he prospered exceedingly; but he thought Reuben's attitude to animals ridiculous, and often said so. If Reuben (Noah said) would only drive his weaker ones into the wilderness and leave them there, he would be able to feed the stronger properly – not just keep them alive by the skin of their teeth, which was all he could afford to do at present.

'He's a good boy, and a kind boy, but he's silly,' Noah often said to his wife, who regularly replied: 'But so good-looking, Noah dear. Not so handsome as Ham, nor so tall, but such a nice smile, and such lovely dark eyes – and if his animals go half-starved the poor young man's at least three-quarter starved himself.'

'Hrrumpth,' said Noah: a plain man's noise.

'And he does try not to starve his wife.'

'Hrrumpth,' said Noah again. He disapproved of Thamar because she was so *very* pretty, much too pretty for an animal-tamer's wife. In her presence he could neither look straight at her, nor away, which made him feel he was about to squint. Ham – he had noticed – simply could not look away. Ham was a worry. He had only been preserved from gold and scarlet and jingling anklets by the firmness of his parents. It was youth – or so Noah, unbelievingly, hoped.

Other things worried him too, just now. He had a feeling there was something wrong, as though a dark cloud hung over all the tribes, even on these days of burning sun and parching thirst and mirages. When he looked at his flocks seeking for scrub grass around his tent, he felt they were somehow threatened. He felt – he didn't know *what* to feel. In the nights he lay awake, and several times lately had been convinced someone wished to speak with him, but when he said questioningly, 'Yes?' into the darkness there was no sound, no flicker of light anywhere; only a strange stillness broken at last by his wife, who floundered gracelessly across the bed, and murmured: 'Noah, have you got a stomach pain? Shall I boil up some water on the watch-fire? If you sip gently it may release the air.'

So now, staring across the plain at Reuben's tent, his worries rose in him again, and erupted into petulance.

'That soft young fool! Just see what he's doing.'

'Why, what is he doing, my Noah?' inquired Noah's wife peaceably from amongst her cooking pots where she was seething lamb in herbs. She was a great seether.

'Hobbling those useless beasts from the South land outside his tent! Silly young idiot! How will he feed them? How will he water them in this tough and thirsty land? Not a hope of rain! He's mad, I tell you – mad.'

Noah's wife sorrowfully clicked her tongue, and seethed.

Noah Receives a Shock

The night came down, and the night wind rustled the tent flap. Otherwise there was silence. Once, before the men in gold and scarlet and anklets had fled away, there had been hubbub at nightfall, singing and shouting, rude songs and ruder words. Now the magnificent starlight showed only the blackness of an empty plain, the pale triangles of Reuben's and Noah's tents facing each other in the dark, and the bulky forms of elephants and camels swaying peaceably as the animals dozed away the night.

Towards the darkest hour, when the wind had dropped, and the stars were clear as diamond chips, Noah woke.

At once he felt the difference: the sense of darkness and hovering threat had gone. The tent was full of penetrating light.

'Rise, Noah, rise and kneel,' said a still small voice speaking to him through the depths of his own mind.

Shaking, Noah rose. His wife snored on, not missing him from beside her. Noah, who was a huge old man, with wildly flowing thick brownish-grey hair and beard, knelt on the hard ground.

'It seems to me,' said the still small voice conversationally, 'that the people are grown exceedingly wild. They worship idols, they take too many wives in marriage and discard those that displease them. They care for nothing and nobody – and they're violent.'

'Indeed, it is so,' admitted Noah.

'Even the animals have grown downright disobedient.

A poor lot, on the whole. I have it in mind to destroy my creation, and make it all over again. I have a distinctly creative urge.'

At this Noah's sense of doom returned. He shook so much he could feel his bones knocking together inside his frame.

'Ah – Lord, Lord!' he stammered.

'A flood,' said the still small voice ruminatively. 'Listen, my servant Noah. For you shall be preserved – you and your wife, and your sons Shem and Japheth, and their wives. Things must continue, after all. Only better.'

'And – and Ham?' pleaded Noah, greatly daring.

There was a pause.

'Ham . . .?' The still small voice was delicately reflective. 'I'm not so sure about Ham.'

Nor was Noah. He tried to turn his thoughts from the boy, in case his mind was read. But it was, of course, quite useless.

'I see we feel alike upon this subject.' The voice spoke gently, so as not to hurt the feelings of a good man and a parent.

'Ham, poor boy,' ventured Noah, 'is not so bad as some, at least he's never worn those anklets – to my knowledge,' he added hastily. 'And his wife – *she* is my favourite daughter-in-law.'

There was a gentle sighing in his ear, which made him feel as though he were being buffeted by a great supernatural storm. 'A clean sweep, that was what I had in mind. Everything mean and small and violent done for. But the zeal of old servants must be rewarded – so take your boy's life, Noah ; but keep a father's eye on him.'

'Lord, you are most gracious.' Noah bowed himself to the ground.

'Remember – a father's eye. And the whole of your mind, Noah, on your great new responsibility. For this is what you are to do . . .'

And in the dark Noah received his instructions; still on his knees, trembling not from cold but from awe, he listened to these orders till the dawn came. Then the inner vision faltered, and faded, while the voice of his wife rose loud and louder like a cock's crow, to exclaim: 'Old man, whatever are you doing? If you cannot come to bed at once I shall never give you goat's curd so late at night again.'

That morning Noah woke late, feeling gigantic not from goat's curd but elation; yet by noon he was very far from happy. For when he told his wife the news – stroking his beard slightly when he came to the complimentary passages about himself – she looked at him oddly and went off to find a weed that, she said, would conquer indigestion or mental confusion. And when he told his sons Shem and Japheth to drop work (Ham seldom worked) and start finding wood to build an Ark, they took so long to obey him that he actually had to go back and bawl them out, and even then he caught them exchanging amused glances, as if they had found him playing with a toy in his dotage. While as for Ham, he laughed so loud and long that Noah had to box his ears not once but five times in all before he stopped.

When his children had at last been brought to a somewhat slowfooted obedience, Noah sat down before his tent and worried. To be laughed at is wretched. To be winked over and sneered about, and have your neighbours go tapping at their heads –

But he had forgotten. There *were* no neighbours. Only Thamar and Reuben.

Thamar! Noah was horrified. Surely there had been some oversight – surely no one so enchanting as Thamar could be destined for a flood? And Reuben was a good boy, if a bit softhearted and stubborn, and with a lamentable tendency to know better than his betters. Noah felt more unhappy and uncomfortable than when Ham's fate had

hung in the balance. Now he shut his eyes against a picture
of Thamar huddled by her husband, rain driving against
them from a black sky empty of sun, and with the water
rising, rising slowly to their waists, and their necks, and
beyond . . .

Then instead of this picture he began to see circles of
colour behind his eyelids, ringing out like ripples on a pond.
Once more there was that penetrating light.

'Yes, Noah?' said the still small voice.

'Ah,' said Noah nervously, 'hrrumpth. I was just wondering if – if there were any orders, any *particular* orders, about
the animal-tamer Reuben and his wife?'

The rings of colour were suddenly agitated as if someone had thrown a stone into the pond. Then they settled
again, even more brilliant than before.

'The future is the future,' said the voice very gently,
'do not try to see into it too far. There is a good reason for
everything that happens – else why should it happen?'

Unable to answer this, Noah bowed himself once more
to the ground in silence. But he couldn't prevent his
thoughts. The boys in anklets might be kittle-cattle, of not
much more value, if one were honest, than the sheep he
killed whenever there was pasture only for a few. But
Thamar –

'Do not try to understand, Noah. Just carry out those
orders. It is enough. And cease to worry, too – your wife
and boys, Shem and Japheth anyway, shall not laugh at
you again.' The rings of colour flickered and faded, and
finally disappeared. Noah was left looking at his present
world: the scrubby landscape with the distant pale tent of
Reuben and Thamar, and the mammoth grey shapes of elephants tethered amongst other animals clustered together
beneath the too-brilliant sky. And in the foreground hurry-
ing towards him, he saw the figure of his wife.

She came to a halt nearby, and he saw that she was trembling. She kept plucking at her sleeve, as if she would pull it up to wipe her hot face, a gesture she often used when cooking. Her fingers shook convulsively.

'Dear me, wife,' said Noah mildly, 'you seem upset. Has something eaten up the weed?'

'Nothing has eaten it,' replied his wife faintly.

'Then what has happened to make you tremble so?'

She swallowed, and shook.

'Come, wife, speak up,' said Noah sharply. He had had a trying time himself.

'As I put out my hand to pluck the weed –' began his wife in a troubled voice, 'there came a sound like the mighty rushing of rain. I was scared, Noah, I remembered what you said. I looked up to heaven, the sun was shining bright as a polished disk in a cloudless sky! But the sound of rain continued, with the wailing of such a wind, although none moved –' she clutched at herself, and faltered.

'Yes?' said Noah, more patiently.

'Then there was a noise like a spear passing by my head,' went on his wife, half-sobbing, 'and a flash of lightning so bright that I shut my eyes. And when – when –'

'*Yes?*'

'When I opened them, all the herbs and the ground beside me were black as woodash. Burned.'

Noah's wife shook and shook. She dropped to her knees with a cry, and prostrated herself before her husband, with her head upon his foot.

'Forgive me for thinking you a stupid old man with a bad stomach, O Noah, favoured above all,' she whispered unsteadily.

'Hrrumpth,' said Noah, puffing out his beard, and generously stroking her head. If it hadn't been for Thamar and Reuben he might have quite enjoyed himself. For the first time in his life he found himself looking forward to Ham's return.

– and Reuben is Dismayed

Reuben had woken that day with a clamping feel of discomfort in his chest. It couldn't be indigestion. Neither he nor Thamar ever ate enough to upset anyone's stomach. Last night they had eaten wild asses' curds, and drunk wild asses' milk, and their insides should have moved to the simple rhythm of a baby's. He should have woken feeling light and free; but as he stretched his arms above his head – carefully, so as not to wake Thamar – the sense of weight persisted.

It was some while before he realized he was just unhappy. Blackly miserable, as he had never been in his whole life. He turned his head to look at the triangular patch of sky which showed where he had pinned back the tent flap the night before so that he and Thamar could watch the stars together. In spite of the small piece he could see of it the day had never looked more beautiful – more clear, brilliant and inviting.

Now that the day had come he could see, too, those other tents in the distance, surrounded by grazing flocks. Noah's habitation and his animals were nothing but a number of shadows on the sandy scrub – lemon-coloured, silverwashed, harmless shadows. Yet after staring at them for a while Reuben knew, deep down and instinctive, that his sense of wretchedness was somehow connected with old man Noah. Kind old man Noah. Good old man Noah. Irritating, very occasionally drunk but usually benevolent, old man Noah.

Well, he wouldn't be drunk at this hour. So he could surely give a sensible answer – but to what?

Reuben slid from Thamar's side, tucked the skin rug back over her, and stood, frowning, just inside the tent. He felt confused. He knew absolutely that there was some very urgent reason why he should go and question Noah. He had an artist's intuitions and he knew that it was so. In the depths of his soul he believed that something dark and hideous and final threatened Thamar, himself, and all the animals. Perhaps it didn't matter much about himself – or even the animals; but it mattered about Thamar. And then, suddenly, he remembered the carved idols of the young men in gold and scarlet, and their arrogance, and he grew very much afraid. Wasn't old man Noah often spoken of with awe as the oracle of the Lord?

Down at the waterhole where the camels drank, Ham was also considering the question of his parent. He sat on the ground, carefully arranged his scarlet robe about him, and directed his young wife to pick up the heavy water-pots and fill them. She was clumsy, because he made her nervous with his cruelty, and today she spilled water on the sand, so that he cursed her for it. Then he drew out a pair of anklets from beneath his robe and tried them on. They jingled with a merry ringing like glass on glass – a piercingly sweet note which gave him much delight.

This pleasure was marred by those intruding thoughts of Noah's latest stupidity, and all the work he had already found for his rebellious son. Ham frowned horribly. The young wife – afterwards she could never tell what had made her do it – picked up the largest waterpot and poured its contents over Ham's feet. The anklets were drowned in a rushing flood. Ham's anger was such, he couldn't speak. He stared at the outrage and, as he stared, the water, seeping away into the sand, for a moment collected in a small pool, a sort of crystal reflecting a small bright-coloured scene. There was the curve of the world's surface against an angry sky. There were the waters covering the earth. There was nothing but storm and rain, waves dark and choppy stretching from horizon to horizon. Resting securely upon them like a cumbrous seabird, battered by storm and alone in a wilderness of water, was a ship of queer design, a wooden house on water, an extraordinary building such as Noah had described. Ham had just time to notice an unhappy camel hanging over the rails, retching, when the water gurgled away into the sand taking the vision with it. For a moment everything was dark and dizzy. Then Ham raised his head and saw his wife's frightened face above him, and beside her stood Reuben who also looked worried, although not as if the worry had much to do with Ham's fainting fit.

'Oh, it's you.' Ham's tone was ungracious, as he mopped at his wet ankles with the end of his scarlet robe. 'What do you want? Fodder for those mangy beasts, I suppose. Well, we've none to spare – and we don't throw what we have away on mountebanks. Why can't you do a job of work?'

Reuben flushed. He never had asked favours of anyone, and Ham's tone was vile.

'You could have earned your bread as a wood and stone carver,' went on Ham, 'but you'd sooner starve with that vulture-food of yours. Living in a dream, playing on a pipe. Workshy, that's you – or so my father says.' Workshy was what Noah called Ham, but Ham saw no reason not to pass it on.

'Carving idols?'

'If people want idols, why not supply them? Simply a question of need. I could have got you unlimited work – for a friendly fee, of course. Anyway, unless you take to wood-carving more often, Thamar will starve. Although she may drown first,' he added, watching Reuben with dark pleasure, 'since my father says she will.'

Reuben gazed at him with all the horror Ham could have wished. '*Noah* says –?'

The cloud of darkness connected with the thought of Noah had come closer.

Ham was smiling.

'My father says that you and Thamar and the tribes, in fact everyone hereabouts but him and Mother and me and my brothers – and our wives and other chattels, of course – are going to drown. And all the animals except two of everything are going to drown, so you can stop bothering about your mangy beasts at once. I should slaughter those monsters you have outside your tent, they might eat well.' Ham shuddered. Being a coward he was heartily afraid of elephants.

Reuben licked his lips, which had gone dry. '*Noah* says –?'

'What my parent says always comes true, because he's such a *good* old man, isn't that right?' Ham laughed sneeringly. The vision in the waterhole had already receded. He longed to punish someone for upsetting him.

'Look at her.' He pointed to his wife. 'Worthless object, skinny, clumsy, fit for nothing.' She began to cry. 'Yet she'll be saved, lucky scrap of garbage, because she's mine. She'll have the privilege of starting life again along with me.'

'Noah hasn't gone mad?' asked Reuben straight out.

'Gone? He is mad. He always was mad. All his generation are mad. All that's needed is to drown *them*,' Ham prodded viciously at the ground, 'and leave people like *me* in charge as Lords of the Universe, and then you'd see something. You may leave us now,' he added, with a gracious wave of the hand, having suddenly remembered that Reuben was only an animal-tamer and not fit company, 'for *I* have work to do. I'm considering a way of collecting two of every wretched animal.' He broke into derisive laughter. No vision could change Ham for more than a minute. His was a nature which found its own level, and it would take most people a good long drop to find it.

('I must say,' said one of the Cherubim who was working on a plan for the new development, 'if Ham's going too it hardly seems worth all the bother and fuss. And the shift in population.'

'You don't imagine any of them are coming up here?' asked a Seraph, lifting up two golden wings in horror.

'Reuben and Thamar?'

The Seraph merely shrugged four of his six magnificent wings, and jiggled four of his golden wheels, and caused a mild whirlwind in the country down below.)

Reuben had not waited for Ham's dismissal. He was already on his way to Noah's tent, where he found Noah's wife peering anxiously out between the flaps, and muttering to herself: 'Two of everything and wood for building, food for eating, firing, doves, drink, where has Ham got to now, oh men are so inconsiderate, not a thing to wear, fancy, a flood –' Privately she had always looked on the Lord God as profoundly masculine in nature.

'Good day.' Reuben's voice was strained. Usually he would have added inside himself 'old Mother Trouble', but by now he was quite as fussed himself as Mother Noah ever was.

'Is it true?' he asked anxiously.

'Is what true?' came a booming voice from the depths of the tent. Noah brushed aside his wife and the tent flaps, and came out into the sunlight, straightening his massive shoulders, his hair and beard like a great brownish flame around his head. His small shrewd eyes, which were generally compassionate, blinked sadly before Reuben's stare.

Noah was wearing the grey penitential robe spattered with ashes that he always wore in oracular mood.

Reuben took one look at the visionary yet practical face, remembered Mother Noah's mumblings, and turned away without speaking or putting the question he had come to ask. He knew Ham had spoken the truth for once; and only time would tell if Noah's latest visions were truth or madness.

Ham Makes a Bargain

'But what is the matter with you, Reuben?'

A hundred times Thamar had asked the question. And a hundred times Reuben shook his head and refused to answer. He couldn't eat; he wouldn't play his pipe; and he paid so little attention to his new elephants that Thamar realized something serious must be wrong. Nothing she could do, however, coaxed the blackness from him. She had known him to have moods before – most musicians do – but never one so bad.

She looked out of the tent hoping to find inspiration farther off, and found it at once.

'Oh Reuben, what a curious thing, here is Noah's second son come to visit us! Could you believe that he would ever stoop so low?' She went off into a peal of laughter, soft, mocking and altogether attractive. It brought Reuben right out of his abstracted fit. He put his arm round her. 'Tell him to go away.'

'Oh Reuben! To go away? I so want to hear what the Lord of all Creation says.'

Reuben gave a groan. He did not want to hear more from Ham, but before he could stop her Thamar had stepped forward and made such a low obeisance that she almost fell over on her entrancing nose. Even Ham was surprised, although it was more or less how he hoped people would behave. He took hold of her joined hands, and raised her in such a gracious manner that Reuben felt an itching in his toe.

'What do you want?' he asked shortly.

Ham raised his handsome eyebrows. 'To talk with you.'

'What about?'

'Alone.'

'I have little time for talk, with all my beasts to tend.'

'Well, I've come to suggest a bargain,' said Ham. 'One that might benefit your wife,' he added meaningly, 'in connection with what I told you yesterday.'

'Oh.' Reuben was thoughtful for a moment. He stared at the ground, and then he said: 'Thamar, beloved: would you water the animals? They are in need of it.'

Behind Ham's back Thamar made an impudent face. Then she performed another deep, graceful obeisance, and almost danced away.

'Your wife is unusually pretty,' said Ham, looking after her.

Reuben's only reply was: 'Come into the tent.'

The two men sat down opposite each other cross-legged on the ground.

At least, Reuben sat. Ham got up again fast, holding his behind and swearing.

'I'm afraid you were sitting on my cat.' Reuben tried his hardest not to smile.

'The savage brute.' Ham was white with rage, and he flexed his strong hands as if he would like to throttle something. The robe which covered his thigh showed five neat puncture marks welling blood.

'Alas, he does not care to be sat on,' explained Reuben, 'since he is not a cushion. Cefalu, come here,' and he caressed the great cat behind his laid-back ears. For once Cefalu did not respond to Reuben's touch. He humped his shoulder muscles and gave Ham an ugly look, and then distinctly spat.

'Oh, Cefalu . . .'

Cefalu lay down with his head towards Reuben and his

tail towards Ham. He was an ugly, thin, muscular cat, with
an unusually long tail. Thamar brushed him so often that
his coat was like thick black plush stretched over a gaunt
frame of wire. There were scars round his head and shoulders. He had fought dogs many times, and won. There was
something insolent about the way the tip of his tail twitched up and down in Ham's direction. If Reuben had not
been there Ham would have drawn his dagger and cut it
off.

'I have come to make a demand and an offer and a bargain,' said Ham. Naturally he put the demand first.

'That's a lot of things to make,' said good-natured
Reuben.

'Either the old man my parent has gone raving mad,
or –' Ham paused to scowl. He was remembering his vision
in the sand.

'Noah is generally right.'

Ham scowled darker than before. He chewed his lip,
stroked his dark beard, and muttered furiously, 'Shem and
Japheth have been sent on a journey to find wood.'

'And animals, I suppose?'

'My revered father has given me a task as well,' sneered
Ham. 'As if I, the one with brains, should occupy my time
collecting animals. That is an animal-tamer's job.'

'Precisely,' agreed Reuben, looking down at his strong,
square hands.

'Anyhow,' went on Ham, 'most of the animals will come.
Just come, by themselves. That is what my father says, and
he is generally –' his sneer was pronounced, 'right.'

'Then I don't see where your difficulty is. You've only
to wait.'

Ham shifted on his puncture marks and regarded Cefalu
with dislike. 'You know my father! He has some fantastic
idea that everyone must work for a passage on this insane
boat of his. He wants cats from Kemi – says they'll never

be allowed to come by themselves – and on the way back he said I could save him trouble and pick up a couple of lions too. Cats from Kemi! Can you see it? Me!'

Cefalu at least couldn't see it. His tail twitched up and down in derision.

Reuben looked grave. In spite of himself a shudder ran up and down his spine – it made him feel as if lightning played on it. Cats from the Black Land! Kemi was the Black Land. Its ancient name came not only from the colour of its Nile-watered soil but from the fear men rightly had of it. That shadowy land to the South-west was also known to them as the Land of the Dead. The hated land, spoken of only in whispers, in tones of superstitious dread – and then men pulled the daggers from their belts and fingered them as though to draw comfort from this protection.

Kemi was the land of many idols, whose gods had terrifying and barbaric names, whose priests ruled with power and dreadful mysteries. The land of cruelty and treachery and slaves – where a man might disappear for the rest of his life and never be seen or heard of again. Kemi, so travellers said, had cities with gorgeous palaces and temples, and tombs reared on the bones of slaves. If Noah were sending Ham down into Kemi, was Reuben's thought, he couldn't have much affection for his son. It was a test of character Ham was destined not to pass. Reuben began to understand the reason for Ham's visit, but did not show that he did.

'The sacred cats of Kemi must be most distinguished animals,' he said in a courteous voice. Cefalu's tail twitched again. This time with jealousy.

'Distinguished – animals!' burst out Ham, and began to swear, jabbing his dagger in and out of the ground close by Cefalu's tail. He called down such frightful and unfilial curses on Noah's head that Reuben sat aghast, almost expecting him to be struck dead. At last Ham ran out of words and stopped. He stared at Reuben, and a sly, cruel smile formed on his lips.

'Only I don't intend to go.'

Reuben was silent.

'And do you know why? Because someone else is going in my stead. You.'

'I do not think so,' said Reuben quietly.

Ham stood up and stuck his thumbs through the girdle round his waist. Now he was enjoying himself. 'A pity,' he said. 'More, a thousand pities – about Thamar, I mean. A beautiful girl, I thought you wouldn't want her to drown.'

Reuben had risen too, and looked him straight in the eyes as he would have looked at a dangerous animal. 'Explain yourself,' he said quietly. It was all he could do not to knock Ham down, take his dagger from him, and –

Ham made a graceful turn or two about the tent, jingling his anklets. He was aware of Reuben's feelings, because he was as sensitive as some very nasty people are, and he enjoyed what he sensed in the young man opposite.

'Come back with a couple of sacred cats from Kemi, and a brace of lions,' he offered, 'and I'll see what can be done about a passage for you and Thamar.'

'You can't do anything, and you wouldn't if you could,' said Reuben surely, but in spite of himself his heart did lighten – till he thought of Kemi, and then it grew dark again. How could he, an ignorant country animal-tamer, a musician, compete with the powerful magician-priests of Kemi for the possession of two sacred cats? A cat can be quite a handful, Reuben knew, even if it has known your ways since birth. *Two* cats –

'Naturally, if the bargain is made and sealed, I shall keep my word,' replied Ham. He drew himself up, very tall and dignified. No one looking at him just then could have guessed how easy he found it to break promises. Reuben preferred not to remember it. At least old man Noah was a monument of truthfulness, and if he later discovered what Ham had promised he might – that is, if he were *allowed* –

So Reuben shut his eyes briefly, for prayer; when he opened them again he saw Ham's scornful stare fixed on him.

'Myself and Thamar; a promise that as many couples as possible will be chosen from my animals; and then I will bring you two lions – and a sacred cat from Kemi.'

'Two cats.'

'Cefalu is a cat,' said Reuben firmly. 'We only need one other.'

Journey Towards Kemi

The departure was at dawn. The great Arabian dawn, which is as if someone spilled a bucket of light over the sleeping world. Reuben on the camel seemed to tower like a black carved figure into the sky, while the camel himself, in bulk and darkness, looked like a mountain, a city, or a sailing ship. Standing where she did in their shadow, and strapping on the water bottles, Thamar could only see her husband as a strange sepia shape against a background of light which was swirling and flowing as if a painter were dashing it across a dark canvas. She had a cold fear that he was being swept away from her – one with the wild magical elements of the world, for ever. Tears fell down her face, but she made no sound. Obedience to harsh reality is learnt early in that country.

'Oh, Reuben, come back safe,' she whispered, and rubbed her face against the camel's woolly hide.

Benoni, the great cream-coloured herd dog, was going too. He stood five paces behind the camel and sniffed the breeze that had risen with the dawn. Who could tell what he learnt from the quivers of his generous, damp nostrils? Far news of lions lying by the kill, waterholes capturing palm reflections and a slice of sky, savage godless tribes on the move – he smelt distant rumours of them all, and his thick tail moved uneasily; and far far beyond the horizon of even a herd dog's senses was the malevolent spicy darkness of the land of Kemi.

Near at hand he could smell a different scent, and the

thick cream-coloured fur rose all along his spine as he recognized the smell of his old friend and enemy, his loved and hated ally Cefalu. There was a hide bag slung over Reuben's shoulder, with a small round hole cut in its base through which poked out the indignant tail of Cefalu, blown up to twice its natural size with fury. You cannot butter a cat's paws on a camel, so the only way to make Cefalu leave home was to bag him, until he was too far out on the journey to desert. Now and then Reuben stroked the bag's outside and murmured soothing words, but the only response was some hoarse spitting noises and the serpentine lashings of an angry tail.

'Farewell, my Thamar,' said Reuben tenderly. He was afraid that unless he went quickly he would never go at all. It would be all too easy to stay safe in his tent like the coward he felt himself to be, safe from the horrors of Kemi and the long uninviting journey, safe in the arms of Thamar; forgetting she was soon to drown. Almost fiercely he urged the camel onward, and Anak the dromedary rolled forward with the light flooding behind him, as a stately ship moves ahead before a steady wind. Cefalu was wriggling, swearing and bumping against Reuben's back, and Benoni trotted behind them like a pale windruffled ghost which the light had not yet swept away.

Thamar turned back toward their tent. She couldn't look at Reuben and Anak and Benoni (and poor bagged Cefalu) growing smaller and smaller as they moved away towards the skyline. Reuben had given her little reason for his journey, which was unusual – normally he told her everything. He had just answered her wistful questions by saying that Ham had given him an errand, and it involved a cat and some lions, and it was a very important one or he would never have gone and left her to manage the animals by herself, wonderful with them though she was: a natural tender of elephants and cosseter of sick donkeys. She was just to stay close, he said, and not listen to gossip – or rather, not listen to anything the Noahs might say –

'But what might the Noahs say?'

'Oh – they might say anything. Like – like, well, that a lot of rain was coming, or –'

'A lot of rain – here!' Thamar threw up her hands and laughed so that the Noahs heard her in their tent. It disturbed old man Noah behind his beard.

When Thamar had finished laughing she said wickedly, with a sideways glance at her husband: 'May I not even gossip with the resplendent Lord Ham?'

'Most certainly not.' Reuben went very red in the face. 'Anyway, he won't be here.'

'You are never going – wherever it *is* you're going – together?' Thamar was pale now, and serious. She knew instinctively that Ham was treacherous.

'No. But Ham is going away.'

'Where?'

'Since when has it been a wife's business to ask questions of her husband?' Reuben spoke roughly to his Thamar for the first time in his life. It was part of the wretched bargain Ham had forced on him that no one should be told that Noah's second son was joining the tribes for some merrymaking – scarlet and anklets – while Reuben stood the terrors of Kemi in his stead, before Noah could enclose his family in virtuous living on the Ark.

At Reuben's words and tone Thamar gasped. Then she had seen the trouble in his face, and threw her arms around his neck and kissed him.

Benoni's coat was thick as a husky's, its purpose to keep out both harsh sun and bitter cold. It was the colour of grain blown flat before the wind. In the scrub-scattered plain, as the sun rose high and higher, he was a shadow of darker creamy gold moving against the gold and silver background. A shadow which moved in the wake of the rangy free-striding camel, or blew suddenly sideways towards entrancing smells, but always headed in a general direction towards the South-west.

At first Reuben, whose thoughts were gloomy and with Thamar, said nothing but rode in silence. Usually he held continual conversations with his beasts – conversations that were not at all one-sided although speech was his alone. He had lived so close to Anak and Benoni and Cefalu that they understood every tone of his voice, each move of his face or body; whereas he in his turn could interpret every mew, growl or camel's coughing grunt, the twitch of a tail, the raising of a paw, the sudden sway of a long neck or irascible humping of an already humped back. Their conversations may as well be fully translated into English here, just as they would be if the animals had used a foreign language.

'This endless sand is getting in my eyes,' said Benoni, as he plodded along. 'There are many miles of it in this direction, O Master. The next waterhole that I can smell is still a long way off, and we will soon be in the desert. Are you certain there can be no mistake?'

'None,' said Reuben shortly. He was homesick already.

'You dogs are stupid creatures,' interposed Anak haughtily, as he weaved his neck from side to side in self-approval. 'You should carry your own supplies, as I do.' He stretched and twitched his nostrils in derision. The water bottles shivered on his back.

'It's well known that camels have water where other people have brains,' spat Cefalu from his sack. He often fought with Benoni, but they were allies against the egotistical camel.

'Ah, is there someone in that bag up there?' Anak wrinkled his disdainful nose, and spat. 'No one would get me inside the dead skin of another animal. But we can't all have principles – why are we taking *you* along, old moth-eaten piece of fur no longer fit for a water bottle?'

Cefalu was torn between a desire to answer back and one to boast. In the end he could not resist saying, his whiskers curled with pride although invisible to the others : 'Are you not aware, my good fool, that this whole expedition is in my honour? When a cat of my standing and warrior nature weds, nothing less than a sacred she-cat will do. We are risking everything, lives and honour and all, to find me a suitable life companion. Naturally, if these sacred she-cats are not all they're said to be, I shall remain tantalizingly single, having inspected the queue of eager brides.'

Anak could not believe this, but nor – since he found the whole expedition odd – could he deny it, so he contented himself with saying : 'You'll be lucky if they stay long enough to be inspected, you failed water bottle.'

'Creatures, hush,' said Reuben wearily. 'There are only four of us, and who knows what dangers we may encounter? We all need each other – only fools quarrel when in danger. As for you, Cefalu –'

'As for me,' rejoined Cefalu tartly, 'my temper might improve if you would let me out of this bag, where I am jolted to jelly by this great miserable hulk of a –'

'Cefalu, quiet. I shall not let you out till the sun is overhead, for if I did you would be off like lightning to Thamar and milk. If you want this sacred bride of yours you must help me catch her, just as Benoni must make a bridge of understanding between us and the lions, later.'

Anak, who had turned back one ear to listen, rolled his bulk derisively from side to side, and snickered. Benoni rushed forward and gripped him by the leg. Anak kicked out and Reuben and Cefalu toppled heavily to the ground.

It was too much. Reuben's black misery surged up within

him. He hated Ham. He hated Kemi. He hated leaving Thamar. For a moment, while he sat rubbing at his bruised head with Anak peering down at him slightly flustered and almost apologetic, he even hated his beloved animals. He cuffed Benoni, all the strength of his arm behind the stroke, across the herd dog's soft sand-coloured muzzle. Such a thing had never happened to one of Reuben's animals before.

After that there was a silence: the small sad silence of man and animals holding their peace was swallowed up in the giant silence all around them. They were all four very still – even Cefalu lay quiet in his bag, his tail stuck straight out behind him. Perhaps he was winded. All the ill-feeling drained slowly out of them, leaving only a sense of the vast impersonality and indifference of the land and sky. At last Reuben rose slowly to his feet. He pulled Benoni towards him and kissed the herd dog on his nose. 'Old friend, never, as long as I live, will I hit you again. It is a promise.' Even Anak was impressed.

Then the camel knelt and Reuben remounted and the four resumed their journey, although now Benoni renounced all frivolous behaviour and kept his nose pointed piously towards his master's back. So they continued on and on, until Thamar and the animals and the Noahs were left so far behind that they might have been a dream in another life. At night the stars shone enormous in a sky so clear that the smallest diamond chip of a shooting star seemed near enough to be touched by a stretched-out hand, while by day the sun was a pitiless circle of fire blenching the landscape to a snow-white dazzle, or a red and shining shield.

At times the horizon darkened ominously – a cloud would hang there, thrown up from the desert instead of formed from out the gigantic bowl of sky. Then Reuben would wrap his ragged burnous close about him, folding it across his face and holding Cefalu – now freed from the bag – closely protected in his arms. Anak sank to his knees – dog and camel lay with their heads pressed close into each other's fur while the flying sand howled towards them across the desert, and reached them in a stinging fury which could have driven the unprotected to madness in half a minute. These storms seldom lasted long. Their lessening could be foretold when the sand ceased to fly horizontally but swirled upwards in twisted silver water-spout columns, and swayed and danced in the returning light of the sun like dervishes.

After such storms there was nothing to tell of the sudden sand-shift which had taken place – the desert was mottled in gold and blue as before, the sky as clear. Only in the centre of the landscape was the small still group of man, dog, cat and kneeling camel, all looking as though they had been moulded out of yellow clay.

A Dangerous Meeting

Long was the journey, many the dangers they encountered. Poisonous snakes, dust-coloured, flickered across the sand – a whisper of death to make Benoni's hackles rise and quiver from his thick ruff to the tip of his tail. (Cefalu was an able snake-killer, yet sometimes even he preferred to stay where he was, his tail like a bottlebrush stuck out beneath Reuben's arm.) Hostile bands of bedouin rode the desert, eyeing the red sands for sight of an easy prey to rob, but by some miracle Reuben and his animals escaped their attention – perhaps Anak was too thin and mangy a camel to arouse their interest. And often at night the air trembled to a lion's roar. Then Benoni would stand, his broad muzzle lifted towards the sound, one ear back, the other cocked inquiringly towards his master, his brown eyes troubled. 'Bring back two of those?' said the look. While Cefalu was heard to remark acidly that it would be plain suicide to have them in the Ark.

'Even a brave man is frightened' says the proverb, 'when he hears his first lion roar.' Reuben, who was brave by nature, had heard the sound many times, but he still drew his burnous close around him, and around Cefalu too, as if it could protect them from the teeth and claws, the terrible mangling bite, of the magnificent desert lord.

Yet another danger greater even than these, because it followed them from one end of the desert to the other, was the fearful spectre of the dry lands: thirst. It seemed at times that Reuben's hide water bottles would never last them for one waterhole until the next. They grew to dread the parched and swollen throat, the burning and blistering which their grim enemy inflicted on his victims. And there was one hideous day when Reuben, journeying by the sun and that sixth sense which men of wilder lands inherit, arrived at a waterhole only to find it close guarded by an armed band of bedouin.

Until night came the four voyagers lay up in the scrub; and then, hidden from their enemy, they turned away, and marched all night with empty water bottles, hoping always to stumble on the up-breaking desert spring that would give them life. But the night passed, the stars went out, and the sun was suddenly in the sky – a globe of terrible power parching them to the bone and turning the desert to a white sheet of cruel, scorching light.

Till noon they marched, with the red motes of dust shooting purple arrows in their eyes. Till their eyes swelled and their throats swelled, and the illusions of madness came to confuse them in grey shapes creeping towards them across the sands, in Thamar hovering with vulture's wings and claws above them, in fountains and gardens and streams of running water clear to their depths. Then – when Anak's woolly hide looked as though cracked by earthquakes and Benoni was carried unconscious across Reuben's knees – another mirage appeared on the horizon.

'Ah, Lord of Lords,' Reuben was muttering between swollen lips, 'how strange we should perish from lack of water – while everyone we know will perish from too much.' He groaned and swayed above Anak's back. 'Grant only that we may die near this beautiful well of water, believing in its truth.' And he urged the camel towards the mirage of palms that stood so enticingly on the horizon. Soon the trees, instead of vanishing, seemed to take on life and substance. The harsh airs blowing off the desert took on a sweeter, moister smell.

'Water,' mewed Cefalu.

'The water of madness,' croaked Reuben.

Anak said nothing. He was better equipped to deal with a waterless life, yet even he felt that shafts of wit at the others' expense would be neither popular nor kind. He set his grey woolly legs towards the date palms; and in a very short time Reuben and Cefalu were lying on their stomachs, drinking and drinking, only stopping to tell each other not to drink too much at once as it might be a bad thing, and drinking again; and then they doused Benoni with water from nose to tail, pouring it on his woolly head and dried-up muzzle until his coat changed from rough gold to sleek greyish-brown. When the herd dog recovered consciousness, and began to lap, Anak lowered his long stiff neck and began filling up too, as only camels can fill.

'Aie – wait a little,' cried Reuben, 'leave some for the water bottles!' Which struck them all as so exquisitely witty that they laughed and laughed until, worn out and reeling with laughter, they fell asleep just where they were.

It was night when they woke. There was no wind, no whisper of palms, and the stars blazed above them while the familiar companions of their nocturnal travels, the galaxies, stood low over the horizon.

'I heard something,' said Reuben.

'I, too,' murmured Benoni, peering eagerly into the distance, 'and it seemed a friendly, a sort of encouraging sound, to me.'

Anak gave a dry cough. 'He who sees friendship everywhere will end in trouble,' he pronounced.

'He who is sour as yesterday's milk has no friends anyway,' muttered Cefalu.

'Be quiet, all of you,' commanded Reuben, 'and listen.'

They listened.

Still some way off there was a muffled sound of many

little hooves striking the ground. There was a tinkling and a jingling, a coughing and a muttering, an occasional low-voiced command. Now, bedouin go silently as shadows; so it dawned on Reuben presently, as he lay flattened with his ear to the ground, that a donkey train, a trading caravan from the North-east, was approaching them. This must mean that they had wandered on to the great North-east trading route to Kemi, which Ham had described to him. He told the others what he thought.

'It leads to the armed forts by the Bitter Lakes,' he explained, 'if I am right. On it are many travellers, and many soldiers going to and from the Black Land.'

'We had better remove from it at once,' said Anak, unfolding off his knees like someone setting up a camera tripod. 'It is asking for trouble, to meet soldiers.'

'They are but men,' said Benoni, 'I bit one, once.'

'They are but men,' scoffed Anak. 'As well say a lion is but a cat.'

'Or a cat is but a mouse with soft paws,' said affronted Cefalu, stretching up full length to sharpen his claws on Anak's offside rear leg as though it were a palm.

Once more Reuben had to restore order.

Now they could hear very plainly the beat of hooves on the hard sand. Out of the darkness came the donkey caravan. Huge ears, and soft, tender muzzles; thin legs tittupping along beneath saddle cloths of red and blue linen, beaded and bobbled and fringed, upon which were perched the most enormous bundles of merchandise Reuben had ever seen. Even by moonlight, a mere half moon, it was possible to see that all the donkeys wore strings of turquoise-coloured beads tied round their necks to protect them from the Evil Eye.

There were many people with the caravan, and guarding both men and donkeys were soldiers. At least, Reuben decided they were soldiers from their air of authority as they pushed everyone around, and the way no one dared complain of being hit or handled roughly by them. These soldiers wore linen kilts, and they were armed with ugly-looking weapons.

In all this crowd of men and animals, however, one person stood out alone. The moment Reuben set eyes on this man going about amongst them all, issuing commands here, requiring attention there, he knew at once they were in the presence of a Personage – someone of importance. And when this man's glance fell on Reuben (whom everyone had overlooked, in the bustle of arrival) he frowned imperiously and made signs to one of his companions, who promptly came over and beckoned Reuben forward.

'Do not go, Master,' croaked Anak, 'I smell danger.'

'You smell donkeys.' Cefalu wrinkled his short nose critically. 'And very like you they smell, too,' he added.

Benoni said nothing, but he too felt apprehensive. He bared his teeth, and growled.

Beneath the Eye

Reuben hesitated. Then he felt the prick of a knife between his shoulderblades, and everything was clear. When he moved forward to confront his summoners words were addressed to him in a voice very used to command. As Reuben could only understand about one in three, he shook his head. For the first time he was hearing the tongue of Kemi.

The personage stared at Reuben, and Reuben stared back. Then a strange, an alarming thing happened to him.

He grew completely terrified. He would have liked to sink to the ground and hide his face against it – in fact, his knees shook so much that he almost fell. He was only conscious of the power in this man – a vast, cold, impersonal power, malignant and hateful, which might at any moment flow towards him like the sea and engulf him.

'You are asked where you come from, and what is your destination?' said another voice at his elbow, in a dialect he could understand, although it was not that of his own tribe. He glanced sideways, and a bright, considering look met his. The questioner was tall, although an unusually slouching stance made him look as though he had been twisted out of shape in a high wind. The head was of normal proportions, the mouth turned downwards at the corners. The expression was apparently sympathetic, yet something about it made Reuben shiver.

'How did you know in what tongue to address me?' he stammered, playing for time.

'I am accustomed to judge a man from his appearance. It is my most useful attribute, to *Them*.' The stranger nodded towards the other man. 'Now, if you would generously answer my question?' he suggested politely; and again there was a movement behind Reuben's back, and again a knife pricked between his shoulderblades.

'I come from the North-east,' he replied shortly, 'where times are hard. And I go now to Kemi, to seek work.'

'So you have friends there? Influence, perhaps?'

'For so short an acquaintance I find your questions very searching,' replied Reuben, as pleasantly as he could; but this reply was ignored, which was extremely rude. Things are not done like this, in that part of the world.

'No doubt you leave a desperate family behind you?'

Reuben was silent, and the pressure between his shoulderblades increased.

'Spies find short living in Kemi,' murmured his questioner, giving what he evidently looked on as a smile; in other words the corners of his downward-curving mouth came upwards into a straight line.

'But I am not a spy.'

'No? Then my questions, which may irritate, can do you no real harm. There are other ways of questioning, of course. More exciting ones.'

'You would threaten me, O interested one?'

'Where important people inquire, it is best to answer.'

'*He* is so important?'

'Aie! You do not recognize his magnificence?'

'You know I am a stranger. A poor man. How should I?'

'What – even a stranger not know the High Priest of Sekhmet, she who dwells in the desert valley, the mighty one, goddess of storm and terror? Lady of Men-nofer?'

'Oh, he is all *that*?' said Reuben thoughtfully. He certainly didn't believe in the powers of false goddesses, but the powers of evil men in this world, material though they may be, can hardly be gainsaid. He did not quite like it. In fact his knees shook again. 'He travels simply, for one so important.'

'You find it sinister? I too – even I, Kenamut, his humble, unworthy interpreter.' An alarming smile, singularly lacking in humility, flashed sideways at Reuben. 'It is said that he who travels with the wind learns much.'

'And he who moves close to the ground, like a serpent, too much,' suggested Reuben, looking thoughtfully at the High Priest, who stared into the distance as though totally detached from the proceedings.

'You appear to have sharp wits, friend,' said Kenamut disagreeably.

'It is by my wits that I earn,' replied Reuben. 'I am a craftsman. A musician. A trainer also of animals.'

'A variety of most useful trades.' The tone made Reuben's flesh creep. Inwardly he cursed Ham. 'In Kemi craftsmen are highly prized by us, if they are truly skilled, and most carefully – looked after. You must permit me to be of help to you in your search; that is, if these influential friends of yours should fail you.'

'I have none, as –' Reuben stopped. He could see from the man's expression that he had fallen into a trap.

'Well, then, it is fortunate, my young friend, that you have met with influential people on your journey, friends who may help you to your object –'

'It is always well to meet true friends,' replied Reuben with dignity, stepping back a pace.

'So, by the next caravan we meet, you should send back a message to your family, in the district of – where did you say?'

'Sir, I do not think I did!' Reuben glanced desperately towards where his animals were huddled together in a little group. He noticed Cefalu was out of sight, crouched behind the camel. 'And if I may now be permitted to –'

'Yes, go – go,' said the other impatiently, waving his hands about in the air. 'You are now part of the caravan. You are beneath the Eye of him who is favoured by the mighty goddess.' And he swivelled what seemed suddenly an immense and terrifying eye in Reuben's direction.

'I do not like their smell,' said Benoni, as Reuben rejoined them.

'Nor I,' growled Cefalu, spitting in the sand.

'It is always folly to speak fair to strangers.' Anak sucked heavily on his yellow teeth.

'As soon as we can give them the slip we must make again for the open desert, waterholes or no waterholes,' was Reuben's decision. 'For I suspect these men of taking slaves. Any excuse would do – that creature who calls himself Kenamut has already pretended to believe I might be spying. I wish we had two more water bottles with us.' He was intensely troubled by his introduction to those who served the myriad dark gods of Kemi. Somehow it made him feel as he did when night fell on the desert – and not a night of stars and moon, either. He took one of his freshly filled water bottles now, and emptied it out on to the sand.

'Why, Master!' said all his animals in unison. They were shocked. In the desert the waste of water is an almost unbelievable sin. Reuben hushed them. 'I need an excuse to see if we are closely watched. Stay all together, and wait for me here.' He took up the empty goatskin, and stepped towards the waterhole.

Immediately, as he had expected, Kenamut was at his side; proof that escape was going to be difficult.

'My dear young friend! Again! In what can I serve you?'

'I would fill my water bottle, before too many animals have drunk.'

'Why, you are a most intelligent young man! Allow me

to accompany you –' Reuben's arm was taken in a formidable grip. 'I fear we shall have to push – you see, we
are almost crowded out already –'

They pushed: until the soldiers recognized Reuben's
companion, and flung themselves hurriedly backwards as if
afraid, taking with them a small band of foreigners; foreign, that is, both to Reuben and to Kemi – Syrians, and
some who spoke a language which marked them as in-
habitants of a far land beyond even the Great Green. These
men had been moving round quite freely – for even a captive need not be guarded heavily in the desert: you have
only to take away his water bottle and he cannot run.

As he filled the goatskin again, Reuben asked: 'Are those
men criminals?'

'Why, no.'

'But nevertheless they are captives of some sort?' persisted Reuben, troubled. 'Are they slaves?'

'My dear friend, you should avoid asking questions to
which the only answer is an awkward one.'

'Does that matter – between friends?'

'Between friends, it is a point. But since I am feeling
tired and far from talkative perhaps you would gratify me
by returning to the company of your beasts, where I can
see you are perfectly at ease? Those soldiers – you may
find them near you – will not trouble you at all. I feel sure
you would not wish me to hurt their feelings by asking
them to move.' The insistent hand clawed at Reuben's arm,
and then he was given a gentle push towards Anak. As he
sat down on the ground beside his animals the soldiers were
settling in a wide circle all around them. Kenamut, straightening his lips in another smile, waved at Reuben in a friendly manner and walked away to join his companion the
High Priest.

Cefalu stuck his head out from beneath the camel's rug,
where he had been sheltering from the night air, gave his

master a worried look, and retreated once again for a cat nap. Anak's long neck quivered as he dozed. Only Benoni, anxious to share Reuben's troubles, poked a soft wet nose into his hand to comfort him.

Cefalu Transfigured

The animals woke at dawn. Reuben, who had only dozed uneasily now and then, didn't have to wake: he just sat up. In one of his dozes he had been back with Thamar, before the elephants arrived and Noah had had his vision. The reality of this dawn was far from comforting. Looking round him he could see the size and extent of the caravan. Even with many of the donkeys almost invisible, lying down amongst those which rested standing up, there seemed to be nothing but a forest of donkeys each way he looked. And far on the outskirts of the resting caravan he could see sentries pacing, upright and spear in hand, at a distance from each other of a mere twenty paces.

Cautiously, in order not to call attention to himself, Reuben opened one of his saddlebags. He drew out a hard meal biscuit, irregularly baked by Thamar, and cut himself a slice of pale sour cheese. Benoni received a piece of salted dried kid. He received it as a good herd dog should, without sniffing or grabbing, held it down between his paws as though he had just captured and killed it, and ate courteously, neither tearing nor gulping, and wiping his muzzle on his paw when he had done. Cefalu, who had made some crabbed remarks about the same piece of kid yesterday, put his head out from under Anak's saddlerug, gazed at Reuben with reproachful eyes, was heard to mutter something about a nice piece of fish two moons ago, and went back in. Anak himself was still asleep. It took much more than dawn, the company of doubtful strangers, and other people's crunchings to wake him up. His head doddered on its long neck like a palm swaying in the wind. There was scurf on his eyelashes, and in the corners of his tightly closed eyes.

Now, as suddenly as the sun had mounted in the sky, the whole camp was in movement – except Anak. Everywhere small brown donkeys, large grey donkeys and thin sand-coloured donkeys were humping themselves to their feet. Donkey drivers were up and tending to their charges. The sentries were being changed efficiently by a fat officer in a kilt. The soldiers who had semi-dozed in a ring around Reuben and his animals were jostling each other with rough jokings and shovings as they prepared food, or baited the other unfortunate captives. In fact a fair-sized space had cleared around the four friends, more from accident than design, and because of the cooking pots' position. The sharp-eyed Kenamut noticed this, and began a meaningful move towards them, as Reuben noted with an anxious heart. It was then that Cefalu, feeling he had hidden his light beneath a bushel long enough, decided to emerge.

He crawled out from beneath the saddlerug and strolled nonchalantly into the middle of that empty space. There he stretched out his front legs before him, so that his chest nearly touched the sand, pointed his back toes very straight like a dancer, erected his tail to a large black exclamation mark, opened his mouth wide to show pink extended tongue and delicately pointed teeth, shut his eyes, and executed a morning stretch exercise which all self-respecting cats do before they start their day.

It is the done thing. Having stretched your back and front paws you then sway forward bolt upright, and stretch your back ones behind you. Thirdly, you hump, like a small bridge. Afterwards there is the business of the morning toilet, which sometimes Cefalu had missed in the desert, because his mouth was dry. However, after all that water the night before, he meant to enjoy a perfect, voluptuous tongue-bath. He was still anticipating this with pleasure, eyes shut, ears laid back, his mouth one continuous yawn, and rocking backwards and forwards from one stretch into another, when he heard the silence. There wasn't so much as a soldier's oath, nor a donkey jingle. Reluctantly he raised his three-cornered eyelids, just to see if everyone had disappeared, and saw something even more astounding.

The whole company of caravanners, not excluding Kenamut and the High Priest, were prostrate in the sand, their heads towards him, their behinds sticking up in the air like Anak's hump. In later life, when he told this story to his grand-kittens, Cefalu always swore he had *not* looked round behind him; that he had known instantly they were doing obeisance to *him*, because all cats know this should happen, though precious few see it. The story even got enhanced as stories will, so that it ended up with his strolling out from the saddlerug knowing what would happen, and performing his stretch exercises with eyes shut simply and charitably so that the poor humans would have time to collect themselves and get down on their faces before lightning of the Great Green Eye in heaven struck them for impiety. Then the most uppity grand-kitten would remark how was it, in that case, that this sort of thing hadn't happened before? And didn't happen now? Which would earn it a clout from a paw and – but that is well in the future.

At the moment we are left with Cefalu trying not to look astounded and succeeding pretty well; Reuben, the only human on his feet, swaying with shock; Benoni smiling all over his muzzle to see his difficult friend's great and unexpected success; Anak flushed deep sand-colour in jealous fury, and muttering that they'd never be able to live this down, not if they went right through Kemi and got lost in the Land Beyond; and the caravanners prostrate, some of them starting to chant and some of them silent, and all with their rumps in the air. While the donkeys, being donkeys, naturally paid no attention to anyone at all, but went on doing what they'd done before, which was nothing.

When he recovered from amazement Cefalu, who like most cats had a streak of pure perversity, played a little game to see how long he could keep his worshippers flat. Something just told him inwardly – later he was to claim clairvoyant powers, but it seems more likely that in a distant past he numbered a cat from Kemi amongst his ancestors – that so long as he continued his morning exercises and toilet, and appeared not to notice anyone, they would remain on their faces. He was right, and it was fun. He took three times as long as usual over his bath, rasping the strawberry-shaped tip of his tongue up and down each leg, twenty times up and down his tail, and very carefully attending to each nook and cranny. Now and then he shot a glance sideways, and it was always gratifying to see those rows of rumps, quivering from strain, sticking up all around. Once, as he attended separately to each whisker, pulling it out and letting it snap back into place, he glanced sideways at Reuben and Benoni and favoured them with a large, triangular wink.

Eventually – when his tail had begun to bore him – he settled himself upright on his narrow black base and faced courteously towards the High Priest, his tail straight out behind him, his ears pricked forward, every line one of gracious condescension and kingly expectation. He looked exactly like those sculptured stone cats which have come down to us from ancient Egypt, and are in our museums till this day.

'We will give audience,' said Cefalu.

Really he gave a small sharp mew, but of course it was instantly understood by the High Priest, who was as versed in cat language as Reuben. Everyone rose, releasing a shower of sand, and the High Priest paced gravely forward and this time prostrated himself at Cefalu's feet, banging his forehead three times on the ground.

'What is your will, O Bast, O Sekhmet?'

Cefalu didn't know why he had acquired these names, but he knew his will, all right.

'A nice piece of fish,' he said firmly, and in spite of himself gave a shiver of anticipation and greedily licked his lips.

The High Priest's firm calves quivered in the sand. If you believe that one or other of your more difficult goddesses has sent a representative, in the shape of a small black cat, into your camp, then it is naturally worrying to turn down her suggestions.

'Great lady, noble wisdom,' the High Priest murmured timorously, 'we are far from the sea, a river, or even a lake. A little goat's milk?'

Cefalu spat.

The High Priest shuddered, and sweat began to gather on his forehead.

'From my own goat?'

Poor Cefalu was suffering a cruel disappointment. He was so hungry, and he did hate salted kid, and goat's milk. He extended his right paw, all the claws out like five neat thorns, and slapped the High Priest indignantly on the forehead. Five small puncture marks began to well blood, as they had once welled on Ham's thigh.

'Oh, Cefalu,' said Reuben automatically.

He created a disturbance. So far as the High Priest went, a welcome one. He rose to his knees, his head erect with indignation, and, pointing at Reuben, uttered a few piercing commands in his own tongue. Four soldiers flung themselves on Reuben and pinioned him. He was bound with thongs, his arms secured behind his back, brought forward, and flung face downwards on the ground.

Benoni, who had attacked the nearest soldier in great

heart and with ravening jaws, had been concussed at once by a tap from a heavy stick, and lay unconscious by Anak's side. Two soldiers were busy trussing him up in a rug and fixing the rough equivalent of a muzzle around his jaws. Anak made no move to come to anyone's aid. He simply lay and observed in a selfish way. It was true there was nothing helpful he could do, but he saw this sooner than most people would have dared. Beneath his sleepy eyelids he was watching the disturbance round Cefalu with keen interest, and busy coining a phrase about 'working quietly for peace in everyone's best interests'.

Sand went up Reuben's nose. He gulped and choked. Cefalu let out a loud indignant mew ('unhand my master') which the High Priest, oddly enough, appeared not to understand. A stream of Kemi speech poured into Reuben's ear and made small sense there. Then Kenamut stood over him, and in a sympathetic voice which belied his evil look, said:

'Are you unaware, O my not-so-intelligent friend, that cats of one colour are sacred to the goddess Bast, and protected by the goddess Sekhmet, and are not to be slackly addressed by common people? Also, I do not think you prostrated yourself when our goddess graciously favoured us. This is punishable in quite an unpleasant way.'

'It's my cat.' Reuben indignantly twisted his head sideways, and spat out some sand. 'He's got nothing to do with any goddess, I assure you. I've had him since he was a kitten – he's a good, warm-hearted, intelligent beast and reliable, but at times requires a firm hand –'

It says something for Cefalu that at this point he again said: 'Unhand my master,' and waved his paw angrily about, but again he was ignored.

'– and the idea of prostrating myself before him is quite unthinkable –' went on Reuben hardily.

At these words Kenamut turned pale. He made a gesture

with his hand, the High Priest nodded, and in a moment four whips were drawn from four soldiers' girdles, and were raised above Reuben to strike. Then Cefalu, suddenly aware that even the favours of a goddess do not always rank as high with her devotees as they should, let out a long mewling cry, gathered his four paws beneath him, and leapt on to his master's back, where he crouched with his jaws drawn up in a spitting snarl, daring the soldiers to come on and do their worst.

This was awkward. There was a brief council of war above the cat and Reuben. Then the whips were lowered and Kenamut said, a little smoother, 'It seems the goddess marks you for her own – whether as sacrifice or slave is not yet quite clear, my young and astonishingly awkward friend.'

The Hovering Hawk

So Reuben was carried down into Kemi on a donkey, his ankles roped together beneath its belly. He was the only captive singled out for this treatment – perhaps his connection with Cefalu, and therefore magic, encouraged Kenamut to keep a watchful eye on him. As a double precaution he was separated from the water bottles, which remained straddle-wise strapped to Anak's hump; and Benoni, who had come round with a large lump on his silky forehead and dizzy as well, was also straddled there, his tail flapping down on one side and his ears on the other. He couldn't think. He could remember nothing of what had happened. And when Cefalu swung past in a litter, born by eight soldiers and lolling amidst furs, he let out a 'woof!' of sheer astonishment.

'So you're back with us again,' said Anak disagreeably out of the corner of his mouth. 'Never thought I'd sink so low as to act as pack camel to a herd dog.'

'My head, oh my head,' moaned Benoni. '*Water* –' His tongue flopped out and licked longingly at the neck of a water bottle just within reach, but his paws were pinioned, and there was no way of getting further than a tantalizing lick; so he gave up, and watched the bright vision of Cefalu sway past below.

'We can *never* go home,' continued Anak, giving a sour belch, and grinding his jaws together as though in pain. 'Not after this. For myself, I shall change my name and live very quietly in the desert seeing no one.'

Benoni groaned. He had just caught sight of Reuben,

some way to the right, plainly a prisoner; and his memory began to return, as though someone were tearing away a fog in shreds and patches, leaving a bright clear picture to emerge.

'They attacked our master,' was all he said to Anak, who moved his long neck in an offended way, and murmured: 'Is this the worst wrong they have done us? You up there on my back – and that old fur water bottle, that swollen-headed bag of bones I've tried to keep in its place since it was a scruffy kitten with a piece of triangular fluff for a tail, that – that *object*, worshipped!' He stopped, annoyed by the heaving of Benoni's furry flanks. 'Of course, if you find it funny . . .'

'Cheer up, poor jealous Anak – in this benighted land we're off to, who knows? They may even worship camels – when I see *you* carried past in a litter –'

Benoni paused to give a sudden moan; for Anak had deliberately humped his hump, which made his passenger feel sick. After that, they continued travelling in silence; Benoni's anxious golden eyes watchful all the time for Reuben, on his donkey, in the crowd.

Their journey was a miserable one. Cefalu alone was well-placed, and he, in spite of his pride and hasty temper, was too good-hearted to enjoy a rise in rank at the others' expense; except, perhaps, Anak's, but as the camel was only suffering from jealous fury Cefalu knew it was unnecessary to waste his pity there, and frequently would lighten his boredom by softly teasing Anak as the litter swung by.

'Cheer up, old friend,' he would call out, 'why so down? If you'll just smile a little, or condescend to cross your legs in some odd camel dance, I'll yet ask for you as slave, and they may hitch you to my litter so that these poor fellows may enjoy a rest.'

However, even Cefalu ran out of witticisms, and all four friends were really too worried for anything but silence. So it was to the sound of strange tongues, and the rapid patter of hooves and jingle of arms, that they marched (or were carried) South-west: first towards richer country near the armed forts by the Bitter Lakes, where they rested up two days, and then on the last lengthy stage of the journey towards Kemi. Often Kenamut walked beside Reuben, politely – or was it cynically? – ignoring his bonds, and would talk of this and that of local interest; such as the famous mountains of Sinaï, which were known as the Turquoise Terraces, because they contained great quantities of that stone which was greatly prized in Kemi, far above emeralds.

Reuben stared dull-eyed at his tormentor. This mockery of conversation was something he could have done without, but he was too proud to show distress. Sometimes he could shut out the terror and dreadfulness of the present by thoughts of Thamar; but even these made things worse in the end, for then he would be haunted by the threat hanging over her, and rage inwardly at Ham. The promised flood would most likely threaten himself and Kemi too, he realized, but this was arid comfort; and in the meantime he was forced to endure Kenamut's company. So on the way there he learnt much about Kemi. Too much. And about slavery too. Things he would never have learnt from anyone else in the caravan, for no one else really understood him when he spoke. These strangers were infinitely more foreign to him than his animals, but from these, his friends, he was separated.

Separated they remained, as well; all four of them. Even Benoni soon recovered, as a tough dog will; was removed from Anak's back, and led muzzled on a rope by one of the High Priest's guards, who had taken a fancy to him. Just once Benoni had tried resistance, sinking back on his furry haunches with all his weight, and dragging the rope collar almost over his head. But he received such a clout for misbehaviour that he decided to obey, at least for the present, and was soon trotting sedately at heel in the dust churned up by the caravan, and always searching from the corner of an anxious amber eye for Reuben on his donkey.

At last, after many weary days and wearier nights of captivity, they crossed a luxuriant valley to a great river, which seemed to them like another sky – a sky ornamented by gorgeous many-oared ships, with huge sails; and heavy cargo boats as well, with penned cattle all staring over the side in mild-eyed amazement at the water.

'What now?' asked Anak haughtily of Cefalu, whose litter had halted nearby. 'Is this the flood our master spoke of? Do these fools and idolaters expect us to swim it? And what indeed is the point, if it is to grow deeper yet?'

'I don't somehow suppose it to be the flood,' answered Cefalu. 'See, the sky is as brilliant as a blue shield. It seems to me a likely place for fish.' And he stretched his limbs one by one, for they tended to cramp now he lived softly, as well as being fatter and softer from lack of exercise.

'What are these great green reeds, I wonder, which rustle importantly as the air stirs them?' murmured Reuben aloud, whose donkey had for once drawn up alongside the camel. Reuben's bound ankles were in poor shape by this time. They showed ugly sores, where flies buzzed and gathered. Yet his had never been a comfortable life, and he was too proud to complain.

'Papyrus,' explained Kenamut, appearing at once, unwanted, beside him. 'The supreme gift of our beautiful river Nile. Of such golden worth is it that here, near the delta, it has become our emblem. We make boats and sandals from the stalks, posts and roofs; we press it crisscrossed into smooth thin sheets for our scribes to write on. We mould cradles of it – and coffins.' Here he drew out

a small knife, pricked Reuben's spine with it, grinned un-
pleasantly, and returned it to its sheath. 'And – while we
are still alive, my dear young friend – we eat the roots.'

'No one gives me a root to eat,' said Cefalu in a dangerous voice; and Kenamut automatically prostrated himself.

'Be patient, O Bast, O Sekhmet,' he murmured placat-
ingly. 'Behold – on the farther bank, the great city of
Men-nofer. And within, your temple.'

'We approve the name Men-nofer,' said Cefalu. 'Its ending – fer – has something pleasing to a cat.'

Nobody answered. As he was now accustomed to vener-
ation this displeased him, so that he looked up to see what
everyone else was staring at.

The caravan had halted all together, and along its flanks
had drawn up other travellers. Here the great North-east
trade-route had reached its appointed end – the ferry path to
Men-nofer. Coming towards them across the wide river,
and moving majestically like a swan on a piece of glass,
was a great green and blue ferry boat with many brown
oarsmen dipping their long oars rhythmically in and out
of the water, to the sound of music.

'We're not going in *that*, I should hope.' Anak disgustedly
wrinkled his lips.

Now the ferry path behind them was jam-packed with
hopeful travellers, and as the boat drew near the bank,
carefully guided in by an expert steersman, the caravan
in its central position was almost pushed forward by
main force into the strip of water now growing rapidly
narrower. . . .

Then the High Priest's guards drew out their heavy whips
and began to flail about them, giving out strange loud cries
and yells which intimidated the pushful travellers and made
them draw back hastily. While in the centre stood forth
the High Priest of Sekhmet, still disguised, yet radiating

power and fat importance to such an extent that the bystanders gave audible gasps of recognition and alarm.

The ferry had reached the shore. The great sun of midday blazed down on them with supernatural splendour as they went aboard. First – bowing slightly from right to left – Cefalu in his litter, with his eight sweating supporters. Then the High Priest of Sekhmet, surrounded by his guards. Next, his interpreter leading Reuben's donkey. And lastly, a draggle of followers, beginning with Anak, Benoni and the other captives, and ending with many heavily-laden little donkeys, saddlebags filled with gold or spice, and merchants and armed soldiers bringing up the rear.

The lowered ramp they mounted was pulled up and made fast again. The more humble travellers were left to gape upon the shore. Steadily, to the sound of chanting, the ship pulled out into the river in a ponderous way, saluted by flocks of waterbirds which rose startled from the papyrus beds, and whirred and flapped and settled again into the comfortable reeds where they had made their homes. The majestic city of Men-nofer was in sight like the shadow of a vast dusky pearl. It hung opalescent before the prisoners' astounded gaze. There was everywhere a lightness, and a brightness, a hint of stately merriment which seemed to belie all they had heard of Kemi. A hawk stood in the sky high above them, as though it would protect the boat beneath its wings. The High Priest joined his hands, and murmured 'Horus', while his guards broke into a song easily identified, from its solemn throb, as a hymn.

For the first time Cefalu felt twinges of disloyalty. Along the shore he had seen several cats hunting with their masters for waterfowl. He relished the comfort of furs beneath his soft fur stomach, while within a gentle rumbling was not unpleasurable, when one looked down into the water – and saw fish darting to and fro beneath. O the lightness and the gaiety of a land where cats went hunting in silver collars, or were worshipped – if of one colour! He found it hard to believe in the darkness of Kemi, and Kemi's gods.

But Reuben had heard of Horus the god, whose symbol was the hawk, and he knew the hawk is cruel. He stared at the dusky pearl of Men-nofer as it expanded and became strings of pearls, and gleaming white obelisks, and shining temples, and a great and daunting palace. In his misery he knew that he should never have risked his hopeless task, which had ended in his being captive on an enemy's barque; no, he should have remained at home near Noah, trying to soften the old man's heart to allow Thamar, at least, upon the Ark.

The papyrus beds they had left behind were now a pale green shadow on a receding shore – a shadow bleached almost silver by the sun. There was music and singing as the ferry boat moved on. The hawk hovered high in the air, protector or menace. And the captives stared miserably towards the scene of their approaching slavery, where the people of Kemi lived not one whit disturbed by the thought of any flood.

Thamar Takes Flight

Nor was Thamar, left all by herself with the other animals, disturbed by it. The only thing that could disturb her, anyway, was Reuben's absence. She had obediently stopped her ears, as he had told her, to any stories she might hear about too much rain. She had to stop them quite often, for Ham tended to look in on her unexpectedly; just to make sure she was all right, he said, trying to take her hand.

With Reuben away Thamar felt very low in spirits, and she hated Ham coming there so often, although she feared to say so in case it offended him and caused trouble for Reuben later on. Yes, she both loathed and distrusted Ham. He wasn't even comic any more, now she was alone and unprotected. So she took to leaving her face unwashed, and her hair unkempt, and rubbed her head often against camel flank or elephant trunk, so that she smelt constantly of animals. But even this didn't prevent Ham's coming, in fact he seemed to take a perverse delight in it, and to come more often, so that she was always glancing up to see his shadow on the sand.

'You look like some wild thing of the desert,' he would say, taking her hand and trying to draw her close to him; and she would pull away, showing her small pointed teeth, and scowl at him, saying: 'I am wild – wild as these dogs of ours.' But this only pleased him more. If it hadn't been for the dogs, and Ham's known cowardice, she would have been very much afraid.

Then one day Ham spoke to her of Reuben's death. Not

as if it might happen, but as though it had, and he was sorry to hurt her; although looking up suddenly she caught a lop-sided grin on his face, and knew he wasn't sorry at all. She wouldn't believe him. She could not. Yet was it possible he had some secret information? Had someone ridden in overnight from the desert with its dread secrets: and then ridden off again too early for her to have seen? She gazed piercingly at Ham, while tears welled in her enormous eyes. He came closer, and again took her hand. She jerked it away. One of the dogs growled, and its eyes went red. Ham shifted ground but did not go away.

'I do not believe you! You lie,' Thamar accused him in a trembling voice. She looked more beautiful than ever, when afraid, and Ham drew a deep excited breath.

'Poor Thamar. Child, it's better to believe bad news quickly, than to hope – and hope, and –' He had been fiddling with a knife. Now he drove it suddenly home in its sheath. Thamar shuddered at the sound. She found herself wondering if it had been a knife, in Reuben's back.... That was the moment when she made up her mind to go and see. The thought was terrible, though nothing like so bad as waiting here, with Ham talking of Reuben's death.

'My wife has also died,' she heard Ham's voice say, with no expression.

'How do you know? You've not been home to your father's tents since Reuben went away.'

'I have my spies. She was always a sickly girl, nothing like so pretty as you. Thamar –' Ham came a step closer. 'Now that Reuben is dead as well, I will take you as my wife.'

Thamar gave a cry as though a snake had bitten her. She shrank backwards, and found herself leaning against an elephant. It had come up quietly – elephants can move without sound when they wish – both because it was, by this time, devoted to Thamar, and because it also distrusted

Ham, who had often teased it and riled it very much when it was feeding. Now, when Ham gave a great tug on Thamar's hand and pulled her towards him, the elephant raised his trunk and lowered it again to box Ham very smartly on either ear.

It was a startling pain. Ham let out a howl of dismay, and leapt nimbly backwards. The amused elephant breathed down Thamar's neck, enveloping her in a cloudy smell of fodder. In spite of her fear, and her despair for Reuben, she couldn't help laughing. Then she stopped. She went cold. Ham's face was wicked. Murderous. With something else –

'When you are my wife, you will regret this.' He spoke very softly, but Thamar shivered and shrank back against the elephant, taking comfort from its huge strength. Ham raised his right hand. The unsheathed knife shone in the brilliant air. He waited just a second too long, pondering where to throw it – at the beast's eye – or –

The elephant's trunk whipped out faster than a striking snake, snatched the knife from Ham's right hand, and flicked it backwards far out of reach. Ham made a sound like a thwarted hyaena; shouted: 'I'll have it slaughtered – and –' his hand made a sweeping gesture, taking in the other animals with the dogs, '– these. I'll have no girl in my tent who stinks of animals.' He choked, glowered, turned on his heel, and strode away. To Thamar's haunted gaze his shadow looked larger and more menacing than when he came. She was still half-supported by the elephant's shoulder. She moaned softly to herself, 'Dead – Reuben is dead,' and felt no pain, only a grey hopelessness which seemed to stretch all round her like the land itself.

The very tip of the elephant's trunk caressed the back of her neck. 'Take heart,' it might have been trying to say.

She put her hand up, explored the pinkish tip like a damp sponge beneath her fingers. After all, she felt safer with the animals and the lonely land than with anything or anyone else except Reuben.

'Come,' she said very quietly to the elephant, closing her fingers round its trunk. 'Perhaps he is not dead after all. Perhaps the Lord Ham lied. We will go and search for him. Yes, that's what we'll do – what we'll all do. Yet first we will sleep – for there may be far to go. And – for secrecy – we will travel by night.'

In spite of fears for Reuben, Thamar slept until night-fall. Gentle and graceful though she was to look at, she was a highly disciplined person. Sleep and food are necessary for strength. When food was short, Thamar slept more. If Reuben was not dead, Thamar would keep up her strength until she found him. If he was really gone from her for ever into a land of shadows, then would be the time to sleep and eat no more, but to lie down and die.

When the moon rose suddenly from beneath the horizon, as though someone had pulled it up like a plummet on the end of a string, Thamar rose too; and the dogs who had slept beside her, guarding her, shook themselves and stretched. Then Thamar and the animals started to break camp. It was the elephants, the latest comers, who were most useful here, for with one twist of a trunk they could pull a tent pole clean out of the ground. Indeed, there was a slight mishap when the female elephant, with too great enterprise, pulled a pole before the others were ready, and in a second a handful of hysterical dogs and the Barbary ape were engulfed together.

However, things were soon sorted out under Thamar's management. The tent, with all Reuben's and Thamar's meagre belongings, was tidily packed away on the male elephant's back, and secured with a hide rope around his stomach. The donkeys were laden with every water-filled hide bottle Thamar could lay her hands on, as well as curd cheeses and thin wine, the herbs and salted kid, and meal, and such fodder as now remained to them since Reuben went away; while the goats bleated together in a silly band.

The dogs were not much help, either. They ran wildly here and there in all directions, their eyes glinting red in the moonlight as they cried in deep-throated voices: 'Let's be off, let's be off,' until Thamar called them to order, formed them into a small pack, and told them very firmly that they were to keep at the elephants' heels and not bother anyone at all, or they would be left behind – when they lay down looking humble and woeful, but ready to jump up again crying: 'Let's be off,' the moment she relented.

Soon there was nothing to show where Reuben and Thamar had had their home except some holes in the sandy soil, where the tent poles had been, already silting up; the spoor of animals; and some animal dung lying around in tidy little heaps ready to be dried and turned into fuel.

Thamar intended to ride the female elephant, who was more obstinate than the male and refused to kneel down because she felt it was beneath her. So Thamar mounted the remaining cream-coloured dromedary, Anak's mate, and transferred herself by means of a jump. Her certainty that no animal could behave meanly towards herself or Reuben caused the elephant to stay quite still, although she was very much annoyed and complained continually, once they had set off, that she was being taken for granted, and wouldn't demean herself, and would lodge a complaint somewhere just as soon as she found out where to lodge it.

As for the Barbary ape, it travelled most comfortably on the dromedary, wrapped up in Reuben's second-best bur-nous, which it generously shared with all its fleas. It looked like a little old desert chieftain, very dried up and burnt black by the sun, as it clutched the scarlet rein tight in its right fist, just as Thamar had shown it, while its great mel-ancholy eyes beneath furrowed brows stared out in wonderment at the endless starry night. When the heavens look as big as they do in that country, a handful of fleas moving around and chatting in low tones can be a comfort, in a homely sort of way.

Noah and his wife were sound asleep in their tent, like sensible people, or they would have been very much surprised, and worried, to see what was happening in Reuben's camp. Noah stirred in his sleep and muttered uneasily, as though he guessed at something. While a distance away, out of sight beyond the horizon, Ham, in the camp of the young men in scarlet with jingling anklets, dreamed of how in the morning he would come with a band of friends and steal Thamar away by force and make her his wife before Reuben, poor fool, could return; if he ever did. And his lips curved into an ugly smile, as in his dream the young men in scarlet yelled wild war-cries, and speared the elephants, and hunted down the dogs before Thamar's terrified gaze. . . .

It was just while this satisfying dream took place that Thamar's caravan set off on the route Reuben had followed earlier. The elephants bulked enormous against the stars and the dog-pack ran in silence behind the donkeys, obedient and keen, with its noses down.

'I shall call you Mouse,' said Thamar to her mount, trying to keep up her own spirits, and patting the grey ridged skin softly and pleasingly with her palm, 'because you are so large, you know.' And the female elephant rumbled her stomach ferociously in disgust, like the sound of distant thunder on a summer's dawn.

Noah in his tent woke for a moment, listened, said: 'I trust that wasn't a herald of the coming rain already, wife,' and settled back to sleep again with an uneasy cannonade of snores; while Mouse's stomach rumbled away towards the horizon, which was dark already with one long unusual streak of cloud.

A High Priest Falls Low

While Thamar's caravan, on the distant start of its journey towards him, was sleeping off the rigours of its start by a waterhole, Reuben was on the point of finding himself in some of the oddest situations ever experienced by a humble animal-tamer who has gone ragged and hungry most of his days, and seen nothing more splendid than the young men in gold and scarlet; and they were hardly impressive to someone who has watched the dry land bloom into a dazzle of bright flowers after rain, and studied the night sky until each star or planet seems like a personal and magnificent friend.

But first, on their arrival in Men-nofer, the four adventurers found themselves truly separated at last. Benoni, struggling on the end of a rope, had accompanied the High Priest's guard, whose name was Ani, to his home in the soldiers' quarter: a square mud-built hut, smelly, full of naked pale brown children like slightly malignant squirrels with inquisitive brown eyes. This hut was only swept out once a week by Ani's wife, a broad-faced woman with masses of black hair falling down over her back and naked breasts, who never spoke except to scold a child or reproach her husband for not bringing back riches from his expeditions. The fact that he had no talent for riches meant nothing to her, for she had long since hardened into a mould of endurance and scornful hate. When she saw Benoni coming she seized a pole with a few bits of reed attached to it which she called a brush, and automatically hit the nearest child on its thin behind.

'Wife,' said Ani pacifically, giving her a nervous smile which got nowhere, 'you have always told me to bring back something of worth from the desert . . .' His words trailed away, and he looked ridiculous. In spite of being an enormous, rather stout man of great muscular strength he was afraid of her. She could be so . . . and then again, she was often . . . as well as being so frequently . . . Yet after all he was a good-natured man who found it hard to dislike anyone, so he stared in admiration at his wife's great bush of hair, and at Benoni with simple love and pride, while all the children gave a great whoop of glee and flung themselves on Benoni like a breaking wave – some twisting his tail to see if it would easily come off, others kissing his muzzle as it uttered pained protests, and one or two, old enough to have all their teeth, sinking them into his ears in the hope they might be good to eat.

Poor Benoni. What more can be said of his new home except that his fortunes seemed as low as they had ever fallen? And when his eyes fell on the stinking goat's bone which his beaming owner offered him, tears trickled down his sandy cheeks and he turned his head away, slightly hampered by the pale brown naked babies who clung to him like burrs. Almost he could have envied Cefalu, whom he had last seen borne in the litter shoulder-high towards a great and splendid temple, while pipes and trumpets shrilled a welcome, and dancing girls undulated laughing before him, clapping their hands, twirling their long kilted skirts, and making happy faces at the crowd – who first prostrated themselves and then began to dance in Cefalu's wake as well.

Anak had also watched Cefalu's welcome, his lips pulled in at the corners in a sardonic smile like a crease in an old leather bag. His smile soon vanished when he found himself led round to the Temple rear to be stabled in a reed-thatched shed with a mass of little donkeys, who one

and all began to bray: 'Spy, stranger, long-neck – go home
to the desert! What do we want with mangy dromedaries?
Only the tribes sink so low as to ride animals so misshapen
– and they hardly ever come to Men-nofer. Go home, ugly
one, go home', and they began to stamp the earthen floor
regularly with their hooves, and to jingle their tasselled
loads, for they were still unsaddled; until their keeper
came in shouting for quiet, and led Anak to a dark railed-
off corner where he could contemplate his shame in peace.
For the first time he began to appreciate Reuben's treatment
of him, and to miss Reuben, and to have faint twinges of
doubt about his own worth and importance in the world.
In fact it was a down-hearted camel who stood sucking his
lips in the dark, wondering if he and his old companions
would ever return to a better way of life.

Reuben himself was the worst off on that first night.
When he was finally released from his donkey, his ankles
unbound, he had stood there swaying, pale beneath his
sun-darkened skin, and even more emaciated than he was
in his half-starved days with Thamar. The High Priest's
guards had jested cruelly while Kenamut stood by eyeing
him with the bright unwinking gaze of the hawk that spies
a succulent young rabbit flattened in terror on the grass.

Reuben's ankles were raw from the rubbing of his bonds,
and his head swam with exhaustion, and fright. Yet he put
all his will into an effort to remain upright and ignore the
brutality he sensed around him; for he felt that anything,
any slight move or act of fear, would unleash it in a tor-
rent of sudden cruelty; senseless violence which might not
be quenched until it left him lying, a limp and useless rag
of bones and blood, on the black and muddy earth – the
ground of Kemi.

In his mind's eye he saw Ham's face grinning at him.
He saw Ham make a threatening, derisive gesture; and

knew inside himself that Thamar was threatened too. This helped him to stay upright, and keep his courage.

The battle of wills proceeded in silence, and in the end Reuben won; won, that is, to the extent of being left alive. An order was given. New shackles were brought – a cuff of metal for his left wrist, another for his ankle, and both joined to a chain, as if he were some sort of tethered beast. Then he was led halting from the yard, through a gateway, and into a formidable-looking square building with small openings high up for light, and a stone like a portcullis which dropped behind them with a clang. He found himself in a long low room scattered ankle-deep in litter and with staples driven at regular intervals into the walls. To each staple was chained some unfortunate prisoner – more violent perhaps than others who thronged the floor, their legs chained together, or their hands manacled behind their backs.

The noise was appalling, until Reuben's guards laid about them with their whips, and then it ceased, to be replaced by whimpers and muttered curses. There was little air in the place, and what there was was foul. There was a smell of unwashed bodies, as well as a worse stench from the open drain which ran down the room's centre. Accustomed to the clean, clear air of wide spaces, Reuben began to retch. This amused his guards hugely. They stood round him, mocking him for his woman's heart. Then they dragged him to the nearest vacant staple, chained him up, and left him with a parting blow and curse.

Reuben paid their departure no attention, nor did the other prisoners pay attention to him. He lay down on the ground and dropped at once into the heavy sleep, almost unconsciousness, of exhaustion, hunger, and despair. Seeing him lie quite still a young rat crept out of the litter and, after watching him cautiously for a while, gently nibbled at a toe to see if it could be good to eat – much as the pale brown babies had nibbled at Benoni's ears.

No sooner had the High Priest of Sekhmet reached his own apartments – after first doing hasty and somewhat absent-minded obeisance to his goddess – than he clapped hands for his slaves and had himself washed and anointed and scented to remove the after effects of travel amongst donkeys, donkeymen and fleas. He did just think of rubbing his chest with oil of lotus, a flagon of which stood always by his bed, marked 'Oil of Pomegranates', but he reconsidered this with a sigh, for oil of lotus was kept traditionally for the kings of Kemi, and as he intended asking for audience once he had eaten he felt it unwise to draw the sensitive royal nostrils his way.

Slaves brought him food in profusion, and exquisite wines as well as his favourite strong rich beer; but he ate and drank sparingly, for a wise man keeps himself and his brain sharpset as a knife when he hopes to cheat his king. While if that king is a god, or believed to be one, it behoves any man of great or little wit to be careful; especially when the god is served by an uncannily astute Vizier.

Even though he ate little and fast the High Priest was interrupted by a royal summons. The King hadn't waited to be asked for audience, but demanded his servant's presence in the throne room immediately. The High Priest cursed (beneath his breath), narrowed his eyes, and wondered which rival priest of another cult had observed his entry to the city, and sent to tell the King. He hoped devoutly, and even prayed automatically to the goddess Sekhmet, that one half of those rich goods in the donkeys' saddlebags had already been safe tucked away in his own treasure house by his discreet and faithful steward.

'I obey the Horus, the Son of Re,' he said shortly; assumed his most splendid necklet with his most treacly and fatherly expression, and, looking like an extremely well-found hippopotamus, had himself conducted behind the King's messenger out of the temple buildings and along the streets to the Palace of White Walls.

On the way he was thinking how much he feared – well, no; not *feared*, exactly: disliked, his great enemy the Vizier, who sometimes seemed curiously more powerful than the frail youth who wore the god-king's double crown; and how much he despised the marshals and court chamberlains, as well as the mischief-making devotees of Hathor – She of the Southern Sycomore; and then he regretted not having eaten a whole roast goose for supper, as well as tiny marshbirds and lettuces, with beer. He thought too of the cat goddess Bast or Bastet, who was specially favoured in the Western quarter of the city, Ankh-Tawy, and wondered if he would finally pass on Cefalu – at a price, considering his magical appearance in the desert – to the younger priests of that cult.

In fact by the time he reached the colonnaded hall outside the throne room he had thought of many things; but not, until this very minute, that he had failed to send an immediate and lavish present to the Vizier.

He clapped a hand to his head; stopped; thought of going back; saw the Vizier coming towards him; knew it was too late – and, scarcely aware of entering the throne room, found himself kissing the dust before the royal feet, while silver trumpets sounded in his ears along with the constant ringing of his own high blood pressure. (Not that he knew it for high blood pressure – he believed himself possessed by a minor deity he had once offended by the Nile.)

'They have let One know,' the Vizier's detested voice was saying smoothly, as the High Priest rose and limped forward puffing to the throne steps, 'that your caravan has returned, O sanctity, with much success.' 'To let One know' was the polite way of saying 'The King has been informed'.

'A little success,' said the High Priest crossly, as he kissed the King's foot and wished they would anoint the young man with a different oil in this hot weather. 'Times are hard,' he added automatically, pulling in his stomach as far as he could which was not very far, 'and tribute not so large as it used to be.'

There was a silence, while the Vizier's eyes seemed to bore into his skull. Drrrr.

The Son of Re, Lord of Diadems, Beloved of Two Ladies (who were the goddesses of North and South), sighed; wished no one had ever invented anything so heavy as a double crown – or at least failed to unite the two kingdoms, whose emblem it was; wished he was in his palace gardens while his singers sang sweetly and the fountains played; wished that crafty old waterpig of a Vizier would *not* harp on the need to build another pyramid (who wants to contemplate his own tomb, when he is less than twenty-two?); wished that all the great men about him didn't look like decayed hippopotamuses, or worse; thought of roses and flamingoes, and exquisite girls, and how much gayer it would feel to be a musician playing to them night and day in the water-gardens, than to sit in a stately gold and white room hung with reed mats and watch his Vizier play cat-and-mouse with a crafty hippopotamus who had cheated him. 'And good luck to him,' thought the Son of Re suddenly – who disliked his Vizier too – 'it must be most exhausting to serve the lion goddess of storm and terror all day long –'

'Not much of a king to look at,' thought the hippopotamus critically. No – the thin neck bent under the crown's weight, the slender body drooped in its simple white kilt. He was frail, and his adam's apple stuck out; but after his death the whole could be remedied by a gold mask, if the sculptor were chosen with care. 'The boy doesn't look like the core of a pyramid,' thought the hippopotamus grouchily, who had not yet taken account of the King's truly remarkable eyes, all-seeing in his pale face. And he began to feel hopeful, which was unwise.

An hour later the High Priest of Sekhmet crept backwards out of the Presence with all his illusions pricked. Instead of an upright man of radiant authority and influence there went out a collapsed bagpipe which has been played on and cast aside.

How could anyone tell, he asked himself, as he leant panting and sweating against a wall, that that devil of a Vizier had secreted two donkeymen – two of his spies – behind the throne pillars, to come forth at the last moment and give the lie to every word he'd said? If the King hadn't been in one of his frequent sweet and lackadaisical moods it would have been an instant journey to the West for such a discredited High Priest. (In Kemi one didn't die, one politely went West.)

As it was, he was condemned to make instant reparation of ten times the amount stolen. Ten times! It would be right down to the bottom of that private treasure house, and start again. It almost seemed that the Vizier – might Set take him to the underworld this very night – knew its contents, and was having a joke at his expense.

The High Priest put his hand up to his neck and wiped away a band of sweat. He was thinking of the crocodiles in the lake, and the labour barracks near the pyramids. Suppose the Vizier was bent on further mischief? The King must be kept in his sweet mood at all costs, or there was no telling what might happen. If only the treasure house held more he would have poured it all, all into the Sun God's hands this very night. He must think of something, and quickly.

But all he could think of, as he crawled slowly homewards, a poverty-stricken old man on shaking legs preceded by his servants, was that the King was passionately, ridiculously fond of music. And a lot of help there was in that.

Meluseth

Cefalu was washing to keep his courage up. He washed three times all over very carefully, gave a hasty look behind him, and began to wash again. It was the first time in his life he had been separated – really separated – from Reuben. And it hadn't dawned on him until his litter had entered the Temple, and the cheering, singing voices of the crowd outside were swallowed by sinister silence, that he was now on his own: just a little cat; nothing to do with any goddess, whether Bast, Bastet or Sekhmet, as he perfectly knew. A black cat of no breeding, softer than he had been from good living, and brought up with a jolt against the bitter fact that for all he knew his master and his friends might soon be dead.

Then again, the litter had been comfortable and gay, and while in it Cefalu had felt quite optimistic. But now his guards had deposited him here, and left him alone in this dark echoing place, this inner sanctuary where stone pillars like huge papyrus reeds soared upwards and were lost to view above; and where the only light was concentrated at one end on something Cefalu preferred not to believe in – an enormous stone-carved female human figure, with a papyrus stem in one hand, and a lion's head. It was certainly the goddess Sekhmet, and she didn't look all that encouraging, thought Cefalu as he bravely washed his tail. His heart drummed in his chest, and he would have made friends with a mouse at that moment and felt the better for it.

He would have to stop washing soon. His tail was quite wet and limp, and his tongue getting dry. If only he could have had a small fire of goat's dung to curl up by he might have felt better, but the stone was icy, and the goddess's expression freezing. 'Well, poor thing, if she's constantly in here night and day –' thought Cefalu frivolously, trying to cheer himself up. Then a long cold shiver went all over him, right from his coal-black tip of nose to the final hair on his tail – in fact every hair not too wet to rise rose on his small body and stood upright like quills on a disturbed porcupine. For out of the corner of his eye, looking where he had not wished to look, he had seen something move. By the goddess's feet. Was it her feet? Was she interested in him? Was she coming over to have a better look – did she perhaps come alive at night and had Reuben been very much mistaken when he laughed about her –

'Wahhhh!' howled Cefalu suddenly in uncontrolled fear, and shot further into the shadows like an uncoiled black spring seeking for a door; but there seemed no way out – not near him, anyhow.

He lay pressed up against the wall, panting. He shut his eyes, because he couldn't bear to look. Then he opened them because he couldn't bear not to look . . .

'I might easily be dead,' he told himself, 'if I had palpitations like that again.' He breathed in and out very cautiously several times to steady himself. Although his eyes were open, he still hadn't looked quite in the direction of the goddess. Or – was she still in that direction? With a great effort he turned his head, and –

The goddess was still in her place. Someone was sitting at her feet; very upright, in the exact position which Cefalu himself had automatically assumed as a sacred cat. A flutter of white in the dimness showed where the most elegant plume of a tail Cefalu had ever seen moved gently to and fro in displeasure. A pair of slightly squinting sapphire eyes reflected whatever light there was in a startling blue beam. They were pure oval in shape, and peered out above singularly beguiling white whiskers – the top ones long and straight, the lower ones retaining an ethereal curve. The rest of this vision was a ball-like cloud of white silk and four paws of melting classic beauty, two of which were out of Cefalu's sight since the vision was sitting on them.

Cefalu's scarred ears pricked forwards. He humped himself ungracefully to his feet – he had humbly given up pretensions to elegance right away – not caring if the vision were celestial or no, and trotted forward hopefully across the floor.

'Come no nearer, stranger,' said a small voice reprovingly from out the cloud of fur. (The voice was rather lost in the fur, which lent it a furry quality all its own.)

Cefalu, obedient for the first time in his life, sat down plop on his backside in the centre of the floor, and brought his tail forward into the second position – that of a cat who is not feeling so sacred as he might.

'We would know why you should trespass in our Temple,' continued the furry voice. A white paw was brought forward, examined critically as if for dust, and returned to its fur harbourage again.

'Are you by any chance the goddess?' asked Cefalu bluntly.

'Goddess?' The vision arched its brows. 'Which goddess?' And it looked round wildly as though to say, 'Where am I?' or 'Are we where I thought I was?'

'That one.' Cefalu nodded over at the statue. 'That one with the lion's head.'

'They've always kept a sort of stone in here,' said the vision vaguely, 'and I've never been so unkind as to make them take it out. This Temple is mine, which I will prove. They bring fish, and leave it as an offering. Who causes it to vanish? I do. They bring fruit, and who rolls it about the floor as though it were a mouse? I. Meat' – she stretched her claws and examined them dispassionately '– disappears in no time, much to the High Priest's surprise. Milk will scarcely stay a moment. And who disturbs the lotus leaves spread on the floor to dry, rustling through them like a cloud –?'

'You?' suggested Cefalu, in the pause.

'Please do not presume on our forced acquaintanceship to interrupt me, sir,' frowned the vision, suddenly sounding rather common. 'I do not propose to notice you again. For I see by the light striking on this stone affair that the moon has risen, and she and I are old friends of all time. She is almost as celestially sacred as am I, which is proved by the way she enters my Temple when she wishes – although she does not share my unusual powers, nor understand all Magic –'

'So did I enter your temple,' said Cefalu boldly, 'therefore I must be celestial too, and may talk with both you and the moon on equal terms.'

He began to pant vulgarly.

'You didn't enter when *you* wished,' said the vision in a knife-edged voice which still held traces of fur about it, 'so I fear this lowly and unfortunate introduction must be disowned completely. If they are intending you to stay, please do not address me again, nor come any nearer; it distresses me very much since it distracts me from most noble thoughts. I am Meluseth, and they call me She Who Loves the Moon.'

She turned her back provocatively, tipping her tail up over it so that every plume was cunningly displayed to best advantage, and appeared lost in a noble dream about the moon – until Cefalu's inquiring nose just touched the outer rim of her silky fur, when she turned with one swift vicious movement, slapped him hard, and as quickly and silently returned to her moonly contemplation.

Cefalu sank back on his haunches a yard away, and stared at her bemused. He had forgotten all about Reuben and Benoni, and Anak – he had even forgotten Thamar, who always nursed him tenderly if he were sick after his many fights. Looking at Meluseth he knew a wild sweet happiness he had never known before. 'Such eyes – such a skin,' he murmured devoutly to himself, 'I'm not fit to touch the tip of her sacred tail.' And he bent forward as though to touch, but thought better of it.

Cefalu had fallen in love, and for the moment all former loyalties were forgotten.

Prisoners and Gods

Reuben woke early. Not because his exhausted body was tired of sleeping, but because in his dreams he knew how much it hurt him. Waking was worse than sleep, however, for all his terrors and problems had been waiting for him like so many vultures. What would become of Thamar, if he could never fight free and get back? Well, that was easy – she would drown. At this thought he turned his face into the filthy litter with a groan.

A large hand descended on his shoulder, and shook him not unkindly, but as though to draw his attention. Reuben took his face out of the muck to see why. He saw a broad-faced man, some two or three years younger than himself, looking down at him. Small, merry, dark eyes were creased at the corners in sympathy.

'Friend,' said a voice in what sounded like a version of his own tongue, 'they deal hardly with you, I fear. I know the men who brought you in – the guards of Sekhmet's High Priest. And it would be my advice to get out of this as quickly as you can.'

'Alas, it seems likely,' said Reuben with a bitter laugh, staring at the staple in the wall. His new acquaintance was only shackled by the legs and could move freely, if shuf-flingly, about the room.

'You must forgive my humour. We have an odd sort in this place. My name is Tahlevi.' The fat man – and he was very fat, Reuben noticed with surprise, for a prisoner – squatted down beside him, and gave a good-natured smile.

Reuben pulled himself up against the wall. 'What brought you here?' He didn't really want to know, his thoughts were still with Thamar; but it seemed polite to ask.

'I am a tomb robber,' said Tahlevi with simple pride, showing his teeth in a fat grin. 'They won't let *me* out of here alive.'

'I wouldn't have thought there could be much to rob in tombs,' suggested Reuben.

'Friend, you don't know these people. A greedy lot. They do nothing but think about what they can store up for use in their afterlife. A look in their tombs would be an eye-opener to you. You see, they believe that if a body is embalmed and hidden safe, then what they call its Ka will never die. While they're about it they provide the Ka with all sorts of things to keep it happy – gold, and food, and slaves, and ornaments – why, the smallest nobleman has a tomb full of pickings, I can tell you.' Tahlevi cracked his fingers hungrily. 'As for the common people like you and me, friend – no offence, I trust – we get shoved in a sand hole and forgotten. No afterlife for us, according to their way of thought.' He gave a pensive grin. 'Why – the sensible thing then is to look well to this one, and a good tomb opened up at night can provide for a whole family.'

Reuben looked at this ingenious young man with amusement. Perhaps he should have been shocked, but some of the poverty he had seen on his way through Kemi – And here were these selfish greedy nobles stuffing their very tombs with gold and food, not caring what happened to other people now or later. Anyway, poor Tahlevi was obviously about to pay a bitter penalty for his crimes.

'Is it so easy?' he asked. 'I should have thought they'd guard these tombs of theirs like gold, if their whole future depends on it.'

'Oh, they do. The trouble is, not all the guards are for their interests. My uncle is a tomb guard.' Tahlevi smiled slyly. 'He sent right out into the desert for me to come and help him.'

'I suppose him dead,' suggested Reuben.

'Why no – he saved his skin at my expense, I fear,' replied the betrayed nephew good-naturedly. 'They were particularly annoyed, you see, because the body had gone too, with all its rings and bracelets. Well – of course one doesn't want a furious Ka hanging round with thoughts of revenge, so one burns the body, and the Ka shrivels up as well. (Another of their strange ideas – still, I like to keep on the safe side.) So someone had to suffer. If I get out of here I shall never trust a relative again, not me.'

'You could have given him away, too.'

'Why – how would that have helped? And besides, a poor old man, always hungry and with sores up both his arms . . .'

Reuben understood that his new friend was good-hearted, and could have been almost cheered by this meeting – if it weren't for Thamar; and his poor scattered friends, the animals.

'Well, they may not kill me after all,' said Tahlevi optimistically. 'There's aways this pyramid for the young King to be built, and as well as many honest labourers who would otherwise starve during the Inundation – the rising of the Nile – there's a slave battalion to which many people like you and me are sent.'

'Isn't that a sure way of killing too?' asked Reuben, concealing a tremor in his voice with difficulty.

'Of course. Around the pyramids they say the grains of sand are not so numerous as human bones,' said Tahlevi frankly and placidly. 'But while one lives there's always hope of escape. As for the pyramids themselves,' he murmured in a longing voice, 'aie – what tombs to crack! If I were free, my friend, I could show you a thing or two I learned from my uncle; my father too, the gods comfort him. But tell me – why are *you* here? You do not look very criminal to me.'

'I hardly know, myself,' Reuben had begun, when he was interrupted. There was a clanging of the portcullis stone. It was being raised. To Reuben's surprise all the free prisoners began to shuffle towards it hopefully.

'Feeding time,' explained Tahlevi hurriedly, getting to his feet. 'Slow starvation time, I should say ...' And he hobbled away with the others.

Under a guard of soldiers three gaolers began carrying in great pitchers of water, which they dumped down in the middle of the floor. Next, huge baskets of evil-looking grey bread were also brought in, and overturned, so that the desperate prisoners fought and scratched and struggled to get a share. No man helped another who was weak, or did anything but fight for himself. No man but Tahlevi, that is. Again and again Reuben saw him carry water in his hands to prisoners who were chained against the wall and so couldn't get within snatching distance of the food. Eventually he reappeared breathlessly at Reuben's side carrying bread for both of them.

'Here – take some of this, if you can chew it. There'll be plenty of water left, presently. Don't expect the gaolers to help you. Watch what they're up to, and let it teach you something of human nature in these parts.'

Reuben was already sinking his teeth into the barley bread, but he turned his head sideways to watch one of the gaolers approach a chained man and offer him bread and water. The man started forward eagerly but the gaoler stopped just out of reach, gave a hearty laugh, poured the water suddenly on the ground, and flung the bread to some-one else. All the soldiers laughed themselves hoarse at this wonderful joke, rolling about, and holding their sides. Then they trooped out, and the portcullis stone clanged into place behind them as they went.

At once Tahlevi took what remained of his own bread and gave it to the man who had been brutally fooled; which made Reuben realize that he was not just naturally good-natured but genuinely good, and he was thankful to have found such a friend.

'You're wondering how I keep so fat, I expect,' said Tahlevi, returning. 'Well, the answer is I've not been here long, no more than the quarter of a moon. Tell me, is that a pipe or some sort of flute I see tucked in your waistband? Can you play a bit? Let's have some music – there's nothing like a few notes, however badly played, to raise one's hopes.' He flung himself down by Reuben's side on the ground, and closed his eyes with a look of almost ludicrous anticipation.

Reuben felt he must show his gratitude, but all the same he drew out his pipe unwillingly. He hadn't blown a note since he was captured – the last time was two nights before he and the animals had made their fatal rendezvous with the caravan. Then he had played a low slumbrous sort of lullaby which had charmed Benoni, set Anak's eyelids drooping and his long neck swaying like a snake, and caused Cefalu to say that it was an admirable sound but nothing to what a well-developed cat could do with his own mouth.

At first, beset in a nostalgic way by memory, Reuben blew very gently and reluctantly: a few notes up, a few notes down. Then in spite of himself the old pleasure took hold of him, and he executed a few delicate runs and half tones. Some prisoners ceased moaning or swearing, and began to listen. Reuben blew on. A silence, except for the thin exquisite music, fell on the prison.

Tahlevi, his eyes still shut, nodded his head in surprise and pleasure. 'Lovely, lovely,' he murmured. The prisoners crept closer, in a ring. Reuben's genius, together with his melancholy, took hold of him, and he played as he had never played before.

The rat, aware that no one was paying it attention, slipped from its hiding place, and began stealthily to gnaw a crust of bread, watching the musician with its bright brown eyes.

The High Priest of Sekhmet also rose with the dawn a worried man. His couch was luxurious, but he hadn't slept so well in it as he usually did, but had tossed and turned, aware of a bump there or a lump here. Since his audience with the King he knew himself changed. Much of the terrible power which had caused Reuben such horror in the desert had seeped out of him, and left him a scared old man. Not that otherwise he was changed for the better overnight. It had been his boast that no slave, man, woman, or child, had ever escaped him, except by death, and you can't sink lower than that – perhaps it's possible to describe evil as the habit of putting your own advantage first, last and all the time before anyone else's feeling or life or death. It was this ruthlessness which Reuben had also sensed about him, and which hadn't altered, except that he was now squashed evil rather than evil rampant.

So the High Priest got out of bed very slowly and reluctantly. Until today he had always risen briskly, with a song on his lips: '*Pup*-pup-pup,' a few notes up and '*pup-pup-pup*' a few notes down, while he remembered that bursting treasure house, and all he would store up in his own mastaba, or tomb. Now he was filled with dismay and he racked his brains, as he had racked them half the night, to think which of his gods he could have offended, to bring him to this pass.

There were so many of them, that was the trouble, he thought despairingly. If you kept up with some, you were bound to be easygoing with others. Many were benign, but some weren't; Particularly if they had a rapacious priesthood behind them like – well, like his own.

The protectors of Kemi slipped into each other, changed names and places, came up behind you when you least expected it. Had he been ungracious with Ptah lately, offhand with Set? You could never tell until the result hit you. Then there were all sorts of others, like the Great White One, a sacred baboon, amongst a myriad of animal gods, and gods with animal heads. There was Anubis, Opener of the Way, the jackal god of embalmers, and Wepwawet the jackal-headed one; and glad indeed was the High Priest that he had never met Wepwawet on a dark night – he preferred his stark old lioness.

Yes – there were gods everywhere. In the sky, in the river, in the funeral or canopic jars. They peeked out from behind trees and went wurra-wurra round tombs. While to crown it all, just lately, the young King had seen in a vision – or said that he had, which amounted to the same thing – the Ka of his dead mother inhabiting a certain tree in the royal gardens, so now the whole court had to prostrate themselves each time they passed it in case the royal lady, who was known in life for her great indignation, had a very great fit of indignation indeed, of a violent psychic sort.

With so much supernatural life going on everywhere it was sometimes difficult to get on with one's own life in peace. It simply *can't* be like this really, the High Priest had often thought rebelliously, when the sun was up and he was feeling lighthearted and young again, and ready to disbelieve in anything, even Sekhmet. But when his stomach gave trouble, or the Vizier threw him a penetrating look, or he passed such a night as he just had – why then, he feared that it could.

He feared it very much this morning. When he was worried he always tended to do actions over and over again in an obsessed way. Now he made a round of his dwelling, paying attention to this god in an alcove here, or that one in a shrine there, then in a panic returning to the first one three times three, and then back to the next six times nine – it was very exhausting, and he feared to leave anyone out.

In order to help his bad memory he had once engraved a small verse in hieroglyphs which went like this:

> Nut – a cow, a sacred cow,
> Re – a god of golden sun,
> Ptah – the word explains itself,
> Ka – will make you long to run ...
> Set – who lords it with the dead,
> Bes – now follows with a flute,
> Bast – a goddess with cat's head,
> Which brings me back to
> Nut.

It was a help, and he was particularly fond of the second line, although sometimes having an uneasy feeling he had got the inspiration from someone else. Perhaps from Sekhmet, in a dream? The only trouble was that it didn't go far enough. Nut, for instance, could be called Hathor too, and it entirely left out hundreds of others, including Isis, Osiris and Horus, although Ptah was another name for –

Here he sat down limply on a chair, and clasped his head. Perhaps if he did all those he'd already done, twelve times four – But then there was Great-Aunt Puzstah. Nothing had been arranged for her, yet –

He peered uneasily out into the garden. Yes, he was right. There was no doubt about it. That tamarisk tree was dying, proof positive that the Ka, or possibly Ba which tended to be bird-headed, of Great-Aunt Puzstah had taken up residence. And still he hadn't made her offerings of any kind. Great-Aunt Puzstah always had followed the royal fashions, however tiresome. Well, he said to himself triumphantly, I'm just not going to let on that I know, that's all. You can flop around that tamarisk till you're dizzy,

Puzstah, and you won't find me with so much as a pomegran-
ate underneath.

But as he went upstairs he began to worry, in case he
should be out there prostrating himself three times three
. . .

He was looking under his couch to see if any minor deity
had taken up residence during the night, when Kenamut's
messenger arrived from Reuben's gaol.

Music Holds the Key

'What do you mean, you can't do anything with them?' asked the High Priest testily. No one of great, if evil, dignity, cares to be found with their rump sticking up, and nervously chirruping at a shadow under a bed.

The messenger knew the signs of a great man's rage all too well. He prostrated himself again, and then crawled near enough to lick the High Priest's toe where it emerged from his sandal. 'Oil of lotus,' he thought, as he ran an experienced tongue round his mouth, 'you'd wonder he'd dare. And out of favour, too,' For rumour passed quickly round Men-nofer as it does in all oriental cities, and grew extra ornaments as it went. It was popularly supposed at the moment that the High Priest's skin had been flayed off him in the King's presence, and now decorated a room in the palace.

The messenger was disappointed to see this was untrue.

'He has bewitched them,' he murmured into the floor.

'Ridiculous.' The High Priest's eyes bulged in his head. He drew back his foot longingly, like someone about to aim at a ball; then let it relax. After all, one must know the truth. 'How could he have bewitched them? If the soldiers cannot get the prisoners out, to work or execution, let them send more in. Don't trouble *me* with the matter when I'm busy.' His eye strayed once more towards the ominous shadow under the bed.

'They *have* sent more in, O great one, O favoured of the goddess.'

'With what result?'

'These too became bewitched, O noble benefactor of the poor.'

The messenger withdrew his face from the neighbourhood of that murderous-looking foot. 'Their eyes do not see, their ears do not hear – that is to say, all they see or hear is the young man.'

'And what does he say to them, this young man of yours – it is the same young man we took prisoner in the desert?'

'He says nothing –'

The eyes narrowed. The voice became both silky and venomous. 'Do you employ your wits to riddle with me, friend?'

The messenger cringed. 'Never, O sun rising on the brow of Sekhmet! The young man plays. He plays a rough instrument, like a flute. He is in rags, and chained, but it is as though Bes walked the earth and played to the poor children of men.'

'Hmmmm,' said the High Priest thoughtfully. A gleam came into his eyes; and he sat down backwards on his couch quite forgetting the shade beneath it. Indeed, at that moment the sun shone into the room with full splendour, filling every darkest corner. This could be looked on as a good sign – while in the tamarisk outside a dove was sitting.

'O Puzstah,' he muttered, 'you have brought me luck.' (Having forgotten his resolve not to notice her.) 'You shall have offerings to spare – but later.'

The messenger was still cringing unhappily on the floor. In his opinion it was a bad sign when they started talking to themselves.

'Be gone,' said the High Priest sharply. 'And do not spread tales about this matter. Tell your master I come to look into it myself.'

With great relief the messenger departed, running

crouched out of the presence like a partridge trying to distract attention from her young.

The High Priest rose, and followed slowly, his head full of plans, and hope.

Outside the gaol there was a little crowd. People were shoving and pushing to get closer. Those at the back were grumbling, and those at the front were shushing, because they couldn't hear Reuben's pipe. The High Priest had most of these people removed from his path by simply sending in his guards, who flailed them to one side or banged their heads together. If one or two heads came off in the process – well, that was life, and particularly life in Kemi. When at last the guards themselves fell silent, bewitched by the sound of Reuben's pipe, the High Priest listened too.

It was as though a bird had got into the prison, and was praising the sun; then the notes changed, and it was the heart of all yearning – Reuben yearning for Thamar. And then, after a pause, the pipe very bravely began a dance, like the dance of creation itself. Reuben had always been a good musician, but it had taken real adversity to perfect his art. Here suddenly it had come to him, and taken possession of him, and he could not stop; and everyone who heard him was turned as still as stone till he had done.

At last – for a piece of hard barley bread and some water give little stamina – he drew the pipe from his lips, and replaced it in his waistband, and realized for the first time that the rat was sitting on his knee.

The moment after he stopped the spell was broken. Reuben grew aware that the High Priest loomed in the doorway, with Kenamut at his side. Everyone else who was standing sank to their knees, and those who were lying rose to theirs. The rat alone was unimpressed, and skipped quickly out of sight behind a water jar.

Tahlevi's kindly face was creased in dismay. He looked

at Reuben, and thought, 'Well, now it is goodbye – they will take him out and cut off his nose and impale him, or some more of their vile work with magic. And he such a good musician, too.'

Reuben himself, with sagging head and flagging heart, thought as well that his last hour was come. He tried hard to feel courageous, but it wasn't easy half-starved and far from home.

The High Priest was looking at him oddly: almost with respect.

Kenamut was looking at him oddly: almost with fear.

Both stared for a moment, then both went away. A second later the High Priest's guards darkened the doorway, came to him, and struck off his chain.

'Goodbye,' said Reuben to Tahlevi, with pale and trembling lips. 'Thank you for feeding me. Here –' He took the pipe from his waistband and gave it to his friend. 'I should like you to have this, for we are not like Them. This possession will never follow me to the next world.'

Tahlevi hardly knew what to say. He looked at Reuben, then at the pipe, with deep emotion. While he was still silent one of the guards fiercely seized his arm, restored the pipe firmly to its owner, bowed very low, and indicated that Reuben was to precede him through the entrance.

'Farewell,' said Reuben.

'Farewell, friend.'

Tahlevi's eyes were troubled as he watched his new friend go. He understood that the guards' behaviour could never be taken at its surface value. With a sigh, he sat patiently down on the floor, gloom creasing his optimistic features. At that moment he felt sure he would never rob a tomb again.

Reuben didn't know what to think, as he was led through the interested crowd to the High Priest's dwelling. Like

Tahlevi he mistrusted everyone around him, and he felt Kenamut might have some fresh unpleasantness in store. On his journey with the caravan he had heard horrific tales about the means of despatch in Kemi – he wondered, with a shudder, how long the barbaric punishment of impalement took to kill.

The High Priest's dwelling was beside the Temple of Sekhmet which had swallowed up Cefalu. Reuben stared at it dull-eyed, and wished he could see his small black friend emerge, head erect, eye bright for mousing, and immensely long tail curved like a candelabra branch. But Cefalu didn't appear, and Reuben, ragged and exhausted, with his ankles bleeding, found himself led through an imposing entrance and a colonnaded hall and then left alone, abandoned to his thoughts, in an anteroom.

He was too exhausted to continue standing, so he sank down on a delicately-carved and elegant stool and stared at the floor.

Soon he heard the sound of soft laughter. He looked up, startled, and saw a girl peering at him round a pillar. There was soft laughter behind him, as well. He turned his head: another girl. He stared at them, bewildered, first one, then the other, and as he did so several other girls entered, with long swinging black hair. They pulled him to his feet, and led him away unresisting. They bathed him, and saw to his wounds. They anointed him – though not with oil of lotus, the High Priest was taking no chances – and dressed him, and put a wig upon his head.

Reuben was far too bewildered to protest, he was their puppet. They stood round him in a circle, clapped their hands, laughed again, for they were always laughing, and bore him, dazed, into the High Priest's presence, where he found Kenamut too.

'My dear young friend!' The interpreter came forward effusively. There was a certain nerviness in his manner, which Reuben put down, quite rightly, to not knowing which side his bread was buttered. 'My remarkably talented young friend – I do trust you will forgive the – ah – certain roughness of your reception in our land. Great men always come to fortune after initiation through trials, is a saying of ours' (he had just made it up), 'and again, many priesthoods enjoin the severest trials on candidates for acceptance to their cult.'

'I have no desire to join any cult of yours,' said Reuben, looking him straight in the eye. A difficult feat when an eye you are looking into keeps shifting.

'Quite so, quite so, indeed.' Kenamut took him by the arm while Reuben tried not to flinch away, and pumped it reassuringly. 'Rest, and drink, and food. That is all you are thinking of at present.'

'No, it's not,' said Reuben. He was thinking of Thamar and the animals; and Tahlevi; and hoping – since we are none of us noble quite all through – that Ham had come to a sticky end; and also wondering if he had got himself into an unpleasant and peculiar dream from which he would shortly wake.

'Food, and drink, and rest,' echoed the High Priest, coming forward on his other side, and giving what he thought of as his heartwarming smile, which had made many people's hearts turn to ice inside them. 'But principally food and drink; then perhaps we might persuade you to give a small musical performance? And then rest. Or dancing girls, if you prefer it.' He dug Reuben in the ribs with an elbow like a stake.

Reuben said nothing. For one thing, he still found it hard to express himself in the tongue of Kemi, although after the lengthy journey he found it easier to understand, because of his quick mind and quicker ear.

The smile left the High Priest's face, to be replaced by a look of anxiety. Reuben was a talented young man; yet it had just crossed his mind that perhaps – considering his connection with the magical cat Cefalu – Reuben was *more* than a talented young man.

'Tell me,' he asked urgently, 'between friends – dear friends – and privately : you are not – Bes?'

'I am just myself,' revealed Reuben simply. He really was quite dizzy by now. He wouldn't have minded some of that food and drink, either. In fact, he was famished.

The High Priest and Kenamut exchanged a glance, which meant : 'Unresolved problem – proceed with caution.'

Between them they urged Reuben towards a table spread with the most delicious food and drink he had ever seen. Fruits of all kinds, sweetmeats, waterfowl spiced and saladed, red wine, golden wine, white wine, sparkling wine –

They sat him down ; they served him themselves. And after an hour or so they even allowed him, fuddled and distended, to have a little sleep, fanned by laughing girls with long swinging black hair, who sang a low and beautiful chant, very different from the High Priest's pup-pup-pup ; although the High Priest *was* pup-pup-pupping in a corner, like a long course of hiccoughs. He was remembering the King's great love of music.

A Cub, a Conquest, and a Reunion

While Reuben slept in luxury, Cefalu loved, Benoni and Anak lived lives of humdrum slavery, and Tahlevi philosophically awaited execution or pyramid labour, Thamar's caravan had gradually slowed up and come to a halt not many stages from where it had set out.

The stimulus that had started it was Ham, and Ham's words about Reuben. Now Ham was left far enough behind for Thamar not to fear him any more, for scornfully she didn't believe him capable of much effort. As for the dreadful rumour of Reuben's death – well, the further she went, the less sure she could be that she was really on his trail. She was now in a little piece of country which was all desert scrub, with numerous waterholes. Reuben could have gone at least five ways from here. Something seemed to nudge at her mind, and tell her to call a halt. She prayed about it, and the nudge remained constant. So here, to wait for Reuben's return or no return, Thamar set up her camp.

It was towards midday, and hot, and she was lying drowsily in her tent, when she heard the dogs begin to bark. At first one, then another, then full chorus. She jumped to her feet and ran outside. The dogs stood in a group, their noses pointing in one direction. The elephants rocked silently, their great ears pushed forward like huge rhubarb leaves. They were listening. The donkeys too were silent, but the goats set up a silly self-important bleat.

Still when Thamar shushed them she could hear nothing. She went over to the dogs.

'What did you hear?'

They grinned at her and wagged their tails.

Thamar frowned. They didn't seem afraid, yet –

She walked forward, cautiously. There she saw it, lying in a huddle on the sandy soil, just in the shade of a thorn bush: a very small lion cub. It looked feeble, with its fur all covered with sweat, and at first Thamar thought it dead. She went over and knelt down by it, putting her hand on its flank, and as she did so could feel a frail panting breath running like a thread through its body.

A great stillness, except for an occasional bleat, brooded over the scrub. And the dogs hadn't been afraid. Nor was Thamar afraid as she picked up the tawny cub and headed back to camp. She felt in her bones that the cub's parents were far away. Either they were dead, or it had been deserted.

Reuben had gone in search of lions and a cat. Here at least she had a lion, to welcome him back when he should come.

In the Temple of Sekhmet at Men-nofer Cefalu was not being quite so faithful to Reuben's memory, for he was much taken up with Meluseth. He had pressed his suit in every way he could think of – and he was a resourceful cat. He had swept lotus leaves into a couch with his tail, and purred round it in an inviting manner. He had caught fat young rats, and geckos, and temptingly displayed them through his whiskers. He had flattered and badgered and stalked and simpered and crooned and wailed and lied. But all he got was a blue glance which looked above his head; the airy wave of a plume as silky hindquarters trotted before him towards a pot of milk or a fish beautifully served with dill on a bed of rushes.

Occasionally Meluseth would condescend to talk. When the moon had gone down, and the Temple was almost dark except for a burning lamp high up on a wall above the goddess, Meluseth would sit with her feet together, and out of the dark would come her small furry voice, talking about herself.

She never spoke direct to Cefalu, but to the air in front of her; yet he would crawl out from behind a pillar, and lie on his stomach listening with hopeless passion to the music of her furry voice, as it went on and on reciting tales of her effect on visitors, the fame of her beauty and understanding, her prowess at hunting, her magic, her superiority to cats past, present and to come, and finally of her power over all living animals which she could bend to her will simply by looking at them. The truth was that she had met few animals, with the exception of some mice, easily crunched up in a single gulp, and Cefalu. Mentally she had crunched him up too. He believed every word she said.

'No wonder they have given her this Temple,' he told himself as he lay stretched out on his admittedly plump stomach near her feet. 'She deserves every inch of it. How magic she is. And how condescending of her to tell me all about it – so like her sweet nature to overcome any nervous fear of boasting, that I may share the benefit of all she is and does.'

From which it may be seen that Cefalu was just like everyone else in love.

He rolled over on his back, and sighed; really, he was getting too fat to be comfortable. There had been many offerings left by the priests lately, and Meluseth, whose fur shape had become quite round, had heroically gone on a diet, drinking only one gift of milk in three, and turning down all else but a little fish. Cefalu, however, had been unable to resist the first luxuries he had ever come across, and he had stuffed and stuffed until he was fat all over except his tail; and then even that had plumped out and turned into a long velvet bolster which took quite a muscular strain to raise.

'I really must stop,' he told himself desperately; but there was just one large pot of cream by that pillar; and then, those three fish on vine leaves were a most engaging shape . . .

'You look too disgusting,' said Meluseth's voice clearly, addressing him directly for only the second time. 'I believe your master starved you. Most cats, of course, don't have a master – they are masters in their own homes. However, it has come to my ears that yours is here in Men-nofer, a prisoner; two of your friends, as well. While all you do is wail that you love me, and stuff stuff stuff yourself full of food. Treacherous, fat, self-indulgent, common beast. Just look at your tail.' She put her small nose in the air and minced past him, swaying her silk hindquarters as she went.

If Cefalu had been more experienced he would have known she was trying to provoke him, and taken heart. Yet he felt a bitter pang, for her words were true. Had he bothered about Benoni, pined thin for Reuben? To tell the truth, he had practically forgotten all about them. He looked at the remaining fish and a half, and felt sick. It was as if his thick plush brush of a tail was filled with black bile. He was ashamed; and in that moment made a triple vow: to diet, like Meluseth; to find his way out of here, back to Reuben; and to take Meluseth with him. After all, she was the sacred cat of Kemi he had come to find.

'What *are* you doing, jumping about like that?' tittered Meluseth, from the perch she had resumed near the goddess's feet. 'You look quite ridiculous, and your stomach wobbles like a dancing girl's.'

Cefalu made no reply as he grimly shadowboxed from right to left, then took a flying jump at a moth, and ran wildly after a leaf as though it were a mouse. He felt all the shame and degradation of his flabby muscles. In spite of Meluseth's mockery he continued grimly to get himself back into training by a jump, a box, and a run.

Benoni was lying in a huddle at the back of the hut. He had retreated there, swept up by Ani's forceful wife. Two or three children had been swept there with him, and lay clutching his cream-coloured – now dirt-coloured – mane, and his tail. He was already accustomed to his tail being sucked for comfort, to never moving without a baby on his back or a pull on his ear. If Reuben hadn't trained him so well there would have been legs bitten all round, and wailing babies. As it was, Benoni concentrated his rage on biting at his fleas. Bite, bite, snuffle, snuffle, first into one shoulder, and then bite, snuffle into the other. It was awful, having fleas (the Barbary ape had kept his to himself), except for the babies, who looked on Benoni's fleas as a new game. Every flea in the quarter seemed to have got into his thick coat, and all the babies stayed quiet for hours, catching them. Even Ani's wife sometimes smiled at Benoni, or threw him an old goat's bone. It was the first time her children had been so quietly occupied.

Ani himself was very proud of his new possession. He brought all his fellow guards to admire Benoni's noble head and bushy coat. He said : 'My dog' to everyone. But Benoni knew he wasn't Ani's dog, he had no intention of being so. He ignored Ani's existence. In vain did Ani tempt him to disloyalty with pieces of goat's bowel, or the lungs of some old horse. Benoni would accept the proffered titbit, then turn his back and patiently deliver himself up to the babies. It was torture, this life, but in the end Reuben would come. He repeated this to himself each hour with less conviction : Reuben would come.

Then at last somebody did come. In haste. Words were gabbled to Ani, whose face fell. He beat his wife for the first time in years – usually she beat him – then between them they dragged Benoni through the streets, and down to the river, where Ani's wife washed out her husband's kilts.

They pushed Benoni in, and held him down, and washed him much the same way, banging him heavily with their hands though not with stones. The fleas popped off in all directions to save themselves from drowning. Mainly they popped on to Ani or his wife, so the whole vicious circle would soon start again. Several babies got washed as well, for the first time in their lives, since they wouldn't be parted from Benoni. Then Ani very sadly took his prized possession, his dog, along to the guardroom, and handed him over to the officer in charge. Who looked at Benoni in horror, and had him washed discreetly from head to tail, and from paw to snout.

Anak had grown so dejected alone in his dark stable – alone, that is, except for the nearby donkeys, who first brayed at him and then forgot him – that he almost went into a decline straight away. He was treated with fair kindness, and fed sometimes and watered, and people came to look at him, for no one kept camels in Men-nofer; but he was exactly the opposite of Cefalu. His bones stuck out and his hump grew more like a molehill and less like a mountain each day. In fact, he had given up hope.

So he could hardly believe it when two little boys came chattering into his stall, groomed him carefully, hung him about with scarlet tasselled harness, placed a string of turquoises around his neck, and led him out into the street; where he saw Benoni coming towards him all one large smile, washed and cleaned and combed till he looked like a gigantic cream fur cushion, and led by an officer on the end of a long scarlet thong.

The Lord of the Two Lands

We must go back now to when Reuben woke from his sleep, which had been made sweet by the fanning and low-voiced singing of the dancing girls. They scattered when they saw him wake, and as if at a pre-arranged signal vanished like so many disturbed lizards through the wide doors.

Reuben sat up and looked around him. He was dazed at first, by this swift change in his circumstances. Then his eye lit on the High Priest, who was lying back on a low couch, watching him in a considering way. Kenamut had disappeared. Reuben thought it was wiser not to put questions, but to wait for answers to reveal themselves. He felt very much better, full of food and wine and sleep. Only his ankles still made him wince, when he moved his legs.

'A-hah,' said the High Priest encouragingly, after a pause.

'A-aahh,' yawned Reuben, before he could stop himself.

'Refreshed, I hope, my dear young guest?'

'Pleasantly,' returned Reuben, with caution.

'Good. Very good. Are you able to stand upright on your legs?'

Reuben tried them. There was a slight wobble, though not noticeable.

'Excellent. Could you manage a short walk? There are some fine gardens close by. We might pay them an informal visit. Fresh air after imprisonment –' The High Priest swung his legs to the ground, and also stood up. His air of power and authority had returned. Reuben found him just as formidable as ever.

He tried a feeble joke, stuttering in Kemi's tongue: 'I th-thought I was to be made a sacrifice.'

The High Priest looked intensely shocked. 'What could have made you think that, my dear young guest? I'm not saying that such things could not happen – If you should turn out in any way disobliging, for instance – But no, we won't talk of it. I am sure you are not an ungracious young man. We will go this way – on informal occasions, I have a path...'

Reuben followed him out of the house by a courtyard, through the garden, and along a narrow alley till they came to a high gate. Soldiers guarded it. They looked doubtfully at the High Priest and his companion, and one man went so far as to mutter a worried comment to another in which the word 'Vizier' could be heard; but owing to the High Priest's bland and challenging stare they were let through.

They found themselves in a magnificent garden, full of exquisite scents, and singing birds. It was formal and yet at the same time cunningly and formally disarranged, so it contained the touch of mystery that gardens ought to have. Reuben thought he had never seen anything more enchanting in his life, particularly after the desert and the dreadful prison; and he longed for Thamar to share it with, and would have lingered, but he was led steadily by path after path as fast as his wobbly legs would carry him. Above towering eucalyptus trees he saw a great white building near, and nearer.

'Did you,' asked the High Priest as they went, 'notice anything unusual about my garden?'

'It was a fine garden,' answered Reuben politely. 'I am no judge of them, never having seen one before that I can remember. It is not quite so beautiful as this.'

'There is a tamarisk in my garden.'

'I saw it.'

'Was there anything in it?' A note of anxiety sounded in the High Priest's voice.

'There was a large bird – a dove, I think.'

'Did she look at you?'

'Yes – and I looked at her.'

'And what did she look like to you?'

'Like a dove.'

'Ah, that's very revealing. Puzstah was always deceptive. She took an interest, did she?'

'Not a very deep one, I think.'

'I daresay she wished to look neutral. She was a most provoking woman, even her legacies made a great deal of trouble, I remember, they were so obscure – Now, as we pass *this* tree, would you mind if we lay down for a brief moment?'

'Not at all,' said Reuben. He was completely at sea, and his legs would be glad of a rest; but it was just like his luck, ever since Ham took a hand in his affairs, he considered gloomily, that he should now find himself in the company of a madman. He lay face downwards and considered an ant nose to nose.

The High Priest rose again, dusting himself, and squinting round him anxiously.

'I don't think there was anyone on the lookout, but one must be careful, and the King is so sensitive – No doves, were there? Or rather, nothing that looked like a dove, and was only pretending?'

'There were three doves up at the top.'

'I cannot really like the sound of that,' said the High Priest gravely. 'There is something going on at court against me, and the King's late mother had two most unpleasant friends – However, one must not jump ahead of events, but keep abreast, keep abreast. Have you your pipe ready? There is probably a slight test coming, and I like to be prepared.'

Reuben politely took the pipe from the waist of his new white linen kilt. His head swam with confusion.

'Now, my dear young guest, I have to explain that to all inquiries you will say you are my slave, my musician.'

'Not your guest?'

'Of course, of course. There is, however, a slight, a subtle distinction between a guest who is a slave, and one who is not, do you understand me?'

Reuben feared that he did.

The High Priest squinted suspiciously at him. 'I hope we may count on it you are *not* Bes? Now it is very unpleasant to be a slave, and very pleasant to be a guest. Whereas a slave who is a guest enjoys, so to speak, the privileges of both worlds. Think about it, my dear young friend, and you will be able to understand exactly what I mean.'

Reuben did, and could.

'Now, when we come into the presence of the King, which I hope to do near here in the watergarden, I shall advance to kiss his feet, while you, some little way behind, will kiss the dust, or, more probably, the grass. You will not rise until you see me make an upward motion of the hand. Any command his Majesty issues will be obeyed instantly.'

'Well, what should I call him?' asked Reuben doubtfully.

'Call him? *Call* him? You will not call the King. The King will call you. When in doubt, kiss the grass. You cannot kiss the grass too often or too thoroughly, particularly if the Vizier is present, which –' said the High Priest plaintively, '– he will be.'

They followed another path in silence. Ahead of them they could now hear voices and laughter. Something within Reuben rebelled at the thought of kissing the grass in front of any king, however important, but he suppressed these feelings for the moment. 'I suppose it's just a custom,' he told himself fiercely, 'and only polite. Though let them try to make me kiss the feet of any goddesses –'

They rounded a corner, and found themselves in the watergarden. As the High Priest had hoped, the King was here, playing with a bevy of outstandingly pretty girls as though they were puppies. He was blowing rose petals at one of them, the prettiest, while his Great Royal Wife, who had lately borne him a sickly son, looked on with a metallic laugh. Near the King stood a man of granite stature, whose legs were as though they had been hewn from trunks of trees. He wore a wide jewelled collar and a sardonic expression.

The High Priest faltered when he saw him, and then twitched his features into a smile which was not returned. He said 'Hah,' beneath his breath, motioned Reuben to follow, and dodged the pretty girls until he could fall ceremoniously on his knees and kiss the royal feet by stretching out his neck. In doing so he intercepted a rose petal, which the King had just blown towards a black-haired beauty of sixteen.

'By Set,' said the King, more seriously disturbed than he had been about the treasure. 'You are an inopportune old man.'

'O my Sovereign, my Lord of Diadems,' said the High Priest hurriedly, 'knowing your Majesty's great love of and gift for music, and how your Majesty complains of your Majesty's musicians –' Here he noticed from the corner of one eye that Reuben was still standing, and made a frantic signal with one foot.

'Senusmet,' the King pointedly addressed his Vizier, 'have my guards yet entered the treasure house of that disgraceful cheat, the High Priest of Sekhmet?'

'The treasure from that impious man's abode is even now in the treasure house of my lord the King,' replied the Vizier smoothly. He was looking at Reuben, who had failed to notice the signalling foot but did notice something so noticeable as the Vizier's stare, and fell rapidly to the ground where he placed his lips against a blade of grass, and did not kiss it.

The King would have liked to ask if his Vizier had kept a fifth or only a twentieth part for himself; but he was young, and still a bit alarmed by Senusmet, who had terrorized the Throne for thirty years. So he returned his attention to the High Priest of Sekhmet who was almost eating the royal toes one by one with every appearance of enjoyment, as though they were the most luscious sweetmeats.

'My Majesty had almost forbidden you my gracious and loving presence,' he said severely, 'and now you disturb my royal pleasures, as you have already disturbed my royal dues. O sanctity, you walk a most dangerous path. I would have you know. And what is this babble about musicians with which you interrupt the royal leisure?'

'It is, I have no doubt at all,' put in Senusmet the Vizier, 'some cunning trick to re-enter the royal approval, and if I were your Majesty –'

'But you are not my Majesty, Senusmet,' returned the King, suddenly finding his courage, 'and I address the guardian of my sister Sekhmet, to whose honour even I owe recognition.'

Very daringly he gave his Vizier look for look. He was growing up. And the Vizier, with a dark scowl and an obsequious bow, made a note of it, and mentally restored to the royal treasury ten parts of the High Priest's treasure he had intended keeping for himself. As he did so his temper boded no good for anyone, and at this moment the blade of grass which had stuck between Reuben's lips let out a shrill squeak. The King jumped. The ladies trilled into surprised laughter. Every toe on the High Priest's feet, already cramped, contracted with anguish.

'A very excellent musician,' said Senusmet, in a grating

voice. 'And a joke at the Sovereign's expense is punishable by –'

'It was an accident,' said Reuben indignantly, raising his gentle and attractive face from the grass. His wig was over one ear. 'No one can breathe normally in this position for very long, it's not humanly possible, nor even dignified.'

The High Priest put his shrinking hands over his ears. 'The boy plays like Bes!' he said in a desperate voice; couldn't hear himself speak; said it again so loudly that as he took his hands from his ears he almost deafened himself.

There was a silence, loud only with birds. The Vizier was gathering his forces for attack. The High Priest was wondering if he would be allowed an elegant supervised suicide, or have to face the crocodiles.

Then the birds were joined by a different sound. It was the King, laughing. 'You monstrous old rogue,' he said to the High Priest, 'stop sweating on my feet. Get up. And you –' he added to Reuben, over his ladies' heads, '– get up and come here.'

The High Priest scrambled thankfully up, bowing, and stood to one side. The ladies parted into two ranks, like the Red Sea dividing, and between them Reuben advanced towards the King. His wig had fallen off, but he hadn't noticed it, he was too interested in his first meeting with royalty. He stood in front of the King, saw what he thought was a very pleasant young man a bit younger than himself, and smiled as man to man. The King's lips twitched.

'Get *down*,' snarled the Vizier.

'Senusmet,' said the King, not even turning his head, 'you may take my pretty Nefru for a walk in the gardens, and do not hurry back. It is a command,' he added, as the Vizier hesitated, 'and you may also take the Great Royal Wife with you if you like, which may stop her laughing; but *go*.'

'I obey my lord the King,' murmured the Vizier between

his teeth; and stalked off clutching the Great Royal Wife with one hand, and the enchanting, reluctant Nefru with the other.

'So you are a musician?' said the King to Reuben.

'Yes, your Majesty. A musician and trainer of performing animals.'

'That is an odd combination.' The King was intrigued. 'And where have you left your animals?'

Reuben's face clouded. 'A long way off, my lord; with my wife. I travelled down to Kemi to seek work,' he added, remembering his original story, 'for times are hard up North. I brought with me only three animals. Now I am the High Priest's musician, and his slave,' he added with a mournful sigh.

'Something else he has stolen from me, no doubt,' said the young King pleasantly, looking at the High Priest, who murmured nervously: 'Indeed, I have hasted to bring the boy as a present to my Sovereign.'

'He would not have troubled with you,' said the King to Reuben, 'if you were not worth while, you can be sure. He hopes you will get him back into my good graces. I wonder if he is right?' The High Priest looked embarrassed. 'So. We will hear you play. Come, my beautiful ones,' and he put his arms round two of the girls, and sat down with them on the rim of a fountain. Drops of crystal water fell all about him and the laughing girls. It was a very pretty scene, and Reuben would have delighted in it if water hadn't reminded him of floods. Anyway, thoughts of Thamar made him forget any self-consciousness he might otherwise have had in playing before a great king, whom his people looked on as a god. Although he could not have been really awestruck, for he thought this king an eminently likeable and reasonable young man. Of course he hadn't yet understood the absolute power which the King enjoyed, although he had seen even the terrible Vizier obey.

He put his pipe to his lips and, thinking dreamily all the time of Thamar, began to blow.

That night, far away from Kemi, Noah looked out of his tent just before lying down to sleep. He was worried. By the disappearance of Thamar with the animals. By the slow progression of the Ark. By thoughts of his boy Ham whom he imagined down in Kemi.

The Ark was still only half accomplished. Its bulk reared up grotesquely out of the soil, a weird sight, black and ominous, a ship out of water. Building had been stopped on it because they had temporarily run out of wood. Some birds and animals had arrived, as though by instinct, and Noah's wife had a hard task looking after them. She was peevish by the time she went to bed.

'What is the matter with you, Noah?' she called fretfully from inside the tent. 'Why can you not come in and settle down, old man?'

'I am looking at the moon,' replied Noah in a gloomy voice.

'And what now is the trouble with the moon?'

'She is looking unusual for the time of year, that is all.'

'How, unusual?'

'The moon', replied Noah in his most prophetic tones, 'is in a cloud.'

Musician to the King

So Reuben became the King's slave, in the palace of the King. He got to know it by its name of White Walls. It was an enchanting place, if you were in the mood for enchantment, which Reuben wasn't. A great many enchantments went on inside it, of both white and black kinds, and worked by the priests of different cults. Reuben grew accustomed to seeing staffs turned into serpents, serpents into staffs. He would come across an enraged priest threatening his rival with a poisonous snake, only to see the rival turn aside the threat by receiving the snake as a deadly hatchet into his own hand.

Through it all the King walked royally attended, but a little aloof, accepting his godhood with faintly smiling lips, and a look of wary amusement in his eyes. He worked hard for his people, dealing out justice, and considering all cases who applied to him personally with zeal and care. He was not greedy, which enraged the Vizier; he preferred to work for what Kemi already had – which was much. In his leisure he loved pretty girls, and music. He was uninterested in plans for his own pyramid, but he was building a temple to the sun god Re, whose son they called him.

What he really thought of himself and his own position, no one knew. What Reuben did know, after playing often for the King's private pleasure, was that the Son of Re could not trust his court, nor love his Great Royal Wife. Unlike so many of his subjects, who were by nature merry, and life- and laughter-loving, the King was sad. The burden of the double crown, the red and white crowns of the North and South, was heavy on him. In his exile Reuben was glad he could a little cheer the King.

And the King was generous. After Reuben's first performance had delighted him, he said to the High Priest, 'Be reinstated in my Majesty's favour, only taking care not to get out of it again.' And to Reuben, 'What can I give you?'

Reuben longed to say 'My freedom', but he knew it was useless. He would sooner be the King's slave than end up again in the unscrupulous hands of the High Priest and his ally Kenamut. So he said: 'My lord the King, please give me back my animals. They are – they were taken from me: my camel Anak, my dog Benoni, and my cat Cefalu.'

The King had arched his brows, and looked at the High Priest piercingly. 'You should learn not to oppress people for nothing, O sanctity! In certain cases it cannot be avoided. But in others – remember that one day your heart will be weighed against a feather in the judgement.' To Reuben, he said: 'They shall be returned to you within days. A man who plays like a god needs all the comfort he can get. I know – being also a god.' But when he heard that Cefalu was already vowed to the goddess Sekhmet, he shook his head. 'Even the King does not offend his sister goddess – for if she is not offended –' he smiled wryly, '– the people will be. Since this animal is in the Temple, there he must stay. Still –' he added noting Reuben's downfallen look, 'on the feast days of Sekhmet, when the court honours the goddess in her Temple, you will certainly see him again. Be sure, at least, he has every comfort there. And a sacred animal is an uneasy possession at the best of times.'

Reuben felt an icy shiver up his spine. He hadn't thought of Temple ceremonies in connection with himself. He would have to get out of going somehow, or he would be made to do obeisance to the goddess; or –!

In either case, he would not see Cefalu again. The King

appeared kind, but Reuben couldn't be sure how he would take the public affronting of his official gods. Although he was at least sure how the High Priest and Vizier would take it – their ways he knew or could guess.

The Vizier, who was so much the High Priest's enemy, showed his hand quite soon.

'My lord the King, the young man's gift is little short of miraculous,' he said, after Reuben had been playing to the court.

The King shot him a quick look. 'That is your opinion, Senusmet? I had not thought you musical.'

'Even the unmusical ear notices when the gods make use of men,' responded the Vizier smoothly.

'True, my Vizier.'

'So, my Sovereign' – Senusmet's eyes met Reuben's like two pebbles – 'the young man should be presented in the Temple of Ptah. A simple dedication.'

The High Priest of Sekhmet made a sudden movement which the King's acute ear noted, though he did not turn his head that way. The High Priest of Ptah, who was also present, smiled from ear to ear as though biting a slice of jucy fruit. 'Indeed, my lord, my most gracious Sovereign, since Ptah is patron of all artisans and artists –' he said eagerly.

The King's eyes narrowed. He looked from priest to priest, who were ruffling up like cocks about to fight, and at the Vizier's face which bore a look of barely-masked satisfaction. Then he studied Reuben, whose hands gripped his pipe unnecessarily, and who had paled.

'Now my Majesty had thought,' said the King agreeably at last, 'that Bes was patron of musicians. But I am over-burdened with cares of state at present, and the cult centre is fatiguingly far –'

Reuben relaxed; too soon.

Senusmet's smooth voice flung another pebble to disturb

the pool: 'Exactly so, my Sovereign. But since it is not wise, for the Two Lands' sake, to offend the gods, and the Temple of Ptah is here at Men-nofer –'

'Senusmet –' the King's voice was even sweeter, 'you are always thoughtful for the kingdoms. You would advise the Son of Re, the Horus, on how not to offend his brother gods? Why, since my father raised you to your exalted position in the Two Lands, you have acquired much wisdom; among other things.'

The court held its breath. Reuben looked at his feet. It is not often one knows the exact moment when one has made an enemy.

In the silence the King rose, and studied his priests and officials with expressionless eyes. For long he had allowed them to bully him, and then suddenly and exhilaratingly he had taken the reins of the state chariot in his two hands, and found, to his delight, it still went forward. Yet he fully understood the dangers he dealt with, and this too exhilarated him. He was on the way to becoming a great man.

'My Majesty will retire,' he said; beckoned Reuben to follow him, and walked slowly from the room. The courtiers and attendant slaves prostrated themselves.

In his own apartment the King flung himself down on a luxuriously draped couch, and sent his servants away. He frowned at Reuben, who had squatted crosslegged on the floor, his pipe in readiness, and said: 'Now what is to be done? They will hunt you like a pack of hyenas. You have become a quarrelling point – worse, a point of honour. I already see three vultures in the sky.'

'While I am the King's personal musician, under the protection of my lord the King?' said Reuben tranquilly. He was playing with Benoni's ears. The herd dog went everywhere at his heels, his silky coat rising slightly in the presence of the High Priest, Kenamut, or the Vizier. Reunion with Benoni had been the high spot of Reuben's success. Anak, whose affections were placid and always self-interested, was content to be within reach, in the royal outbuildings.

'Is a Temple dedication such great matter?' asked the King looking intently at him. 'It is a mere everyday form.'

Reuben's hand on Benoni's head was suddenly still.

'Yes, my lord. I should –' he swallowed, 'have to refuse.'

'Re-fuse?'

Reuben felt a constriction in his throat.

'Yes, your Majesty.'

'I wonder,' said the King's voice pleasantly, almost absently, 'if you have quite understood the extent of my powers, being but a peasant from another land.'

'My lord the King, I –'

'Or that you are now my slave?'

'Your Majesty, I do, but –'

'Be silent.'

Benoni sat up and a growl vibrated in his throat like a rattle. The horrified Reuben put a hand on his forehead and pushed him down.

'Your dog does not appear to realize it, at least.' Reuben was unsure if there was amusement in the deliberately pleasant voice. He began to sweat. 'What if I tell you now to come here and kiss the ground before my feet because I am a god?'

Reuben flushed, and swallowed again. 'I would kiss the ground before your Majesty's feet because you are a great king, and you have been good to me, and have rescued me from death. But not because you are a god. Your power comes from the true God, and it is not your own.'

'By Osiris himself!' The young King sat up, staring. 'It is easy to see you were not born in Egypt, my friend. Have you not heard of beatings, of crocodiles, of disfigurements and dismemberments and impalements? Do they not make you shudder?'

'Yes, my lord the King,' said Reuben, shivering. 'I have – and they do.'

'Reuben,' said the King very softly, 'come here and kiss the ground before my feet.'

'Because your Majesty is a god?' asked Reuben soberly, not moving.

'No. Because I am king in Egypt, and you have been more impertinent than any man in my kingdom – and lived.'

'Yes,' said the King, after Reuben had willingly prostrated himself, 'and Benoni had better learn to kiss the ground as well, because if he makes any more noises in his throat like that I will have him banned the palace. I have enough on my immortal mind without having the royal calves threatened.'

'Your Majesty remembers that he has not yet had a chance to sniff your Majesty?' said Reuben tentatively.

The King cast up his eyes. 'It is good my Vizier is not present,' he said palely. 'Permission is given to sniff.'

So Benoni was cautiously advanced to sniff the royal hands. After consideration he was seen to wag his tail, first dubiously, then faster, and after that he licked hands thoroughly on appointment.

'My Majesty is indeed relieved', said the King coldly, observing that Reuben was suppressing laughter, 'that Benoni feels I should retain my throne at present. By Ourself the Horus, if you were not so excellent a musician you should both entertain the crocodiles tomorrow! But I need hardly bother, since one of my great men will certainly have you impaled before you are done.'

'Will not my lord the King protect me with his justice?' suggested Reuben, recovering Benoni, who seemed bent on sharing the royal couch.

The King looked at him very sadly. 'Justice? Justice is almost always the first casualty in affairs of state.'

'But your Majesty has just told me of your Majesty's power.'

'All my subjects, including my most noble Vizier,' said the King wryly, 'acknowledge and willingly aid my power for doing harm. It is when I exert it for the common good that the trial begins.'

'I am sorry.' Reuben spoke with kindly sincerity. 'Does your Majesty have a true belief in all these gods of yours?'

'Reuben, I find your simplicity overwhelming. You play your way into the presence, and suppose it entitles you to put innocent questions! At least be warned, and do not put them to anyone else. I would like to see my Vizier's face, though.' The King sighed, longingly. 'One does not willingly offend a person, so why should one willingly offend a god, if one cannot disprove his – or her – existence? The sun at least is a great power. Until we are dead, we cannot know what lies behind the sun.'

Reuben looked at the King, and felt what he always had in his presence – kinship with him; and pity. It was curious, because he was now a slave, while the King was mighty in wealth and grandeur, and had power of life or death over him. On the face of it, no two people could have been called more unequal in destiny. Yet Reuben guessed it was not so that the King would talk to many others round him. Perhaps he felt that to talk with a slave was to talk to no one.

'You are silent, my musician.'

'I was wondering how your Majesty came to talk so freely to me.'

The King smiled faintly. 'I also wonder. It is unusual. I can have you silenced by a crocodile whenever I choose, of course. You are smiling, my friend. You do not believe me?'

'Your Majesty has the power.'

'But you also believe in the softness of my heart. So does not my High Priest of Sekhmet! Kings do not have hearts,

Reuben. They are made of granite or limestone, like their tombs. And their wives are made of gold, like the palace furniture. And their courtiers are polished ivory – and greed.'

'Does your Majesty not love your wife then?' asked Reuben bluntly.

'Another innocent question! My Great Royal Wife is my sister. As a sister I did not object to her. The others – well, they are pretty enough. I love them for their prettiness – but it is easier to remember Benoni. He at least is unique.' The King looked at Reuben mockingly, but did not like what he saw there, and his face froze. He said, like an angry boy, 'Do not have the impertinence to pity me, or I will have you whipped.'

'I am sorry, your Majesty.'

After a moment the King bit his lip, and laughed shortly. 'How many loving wives did you leave behind you in your country?'

'One, my lord the King.'

'She will grow tired of expecting you back.'

'No, she would never grow tired.'

'You are to be envied. My wives would tire soon enough of me, if I could not load them with jewels.' The King sighed. 'Why do you not ask me for your freedom?'

'Your Majesty would not give it.'

'And how do you know that?'

'Because if your Majesty did, the moment I was far enough off from the palace for it not to reach your Majesty's ears, I would be captured again.'

'Reuben, you are growing astute in the atmosphere of my court. Anyway, I should not release you. Your skill as a musician lightens my care. I have never had one to equal you – no, nor near it.'

'I am content to be your Majesty's musician,' said Reuben equably.

'Until you escape, you mean.' The King looked hard at him. 'I would not try it, if I were you.'

'Now did I tell your Majesty that I should try it?'

'No. I read it in your too great acceptance. Remember your life in gaol. Also remember that I cannot protect you outside this palace, and there are other – and worse – men who employ slaves as musicians. They tell me too many lies and I cannot see what goes on.'

The word gaol had made Reuben think of Tahlevi again. He had thought of him often, and wondered if he dare try for his release; but he knew how tomb robbers were treated, and so he had feared that attention drawn to Tahlevi might send him to his punishment without delay. However, the King had subtly revealed his own uncertain beliefs. Reuben looked at him, and hesitated.

'What now?' asked the King.

'My lord, I have been thinking much about a man who was kind to me in prison, and wondering –'

'If I would release him as a reward for your playing? What crime had he committed?'

'Well,' said Reuben, conscious of the need for carefulness, 'I believe that he stole.'

Unfortunately the King was astute. 'He was not a tomb robber? So many of them are.'

'My lord the King, I believe he was,' said Reuben reluctantly.

'And his name?'

'Tahlevi.'

The King raised his hands in horror, with the ghost of a laugh. 'Do not mention it! It has boomed every day in my ears for the past moon, with resounding indignation. It was my Majesty's devoted servant Senusmet's mother's tomb that was so lightheartedly excavated.' He looked at Reuben sardonically. 'Yes – you agree: it was unwise. If I allowed this man to go unpunished it would so gravely offend my

most efficient Vizier that the smooth running of the Two
Lands would be in danger. You see, Senusmet's mother is –
missing. The impalement will be in two days' time – publicly. The man is already counted dead.'

Reuben stared down at Benoni, who was lying in a sphinx-
like position across his feet. His heart felt like lead. Kemi
was just as terrible as he had always heard. While he was
thinking so he was absently fingering his pipe –

'Play, Reuben,' said the King.

Reuben looked up. The King's face was rigidly white.

'Yes,' said the King, watching him. 'Life is hard, Reuben,
and death is worse ; and kings, as I told you, must be granite.
Play.'

The Golden Goddess

The day when the robber of the Vizier's mother's tomb was to be executed was decreed a public holiday. It was said that though the Sovereign, the Lord of the Two Lands, would not watch the actual execution, he would certainly go in procession to the Temple of Ptah. The shops would close. Everyone agreed it was a great honour for Tahlevi, since such scum were usually despatched carelessly in some dark corner or other, while this time the Vizier himself intended to gloat publicly on the spectacle. Everywhere mothers began to groom their children for the occasion, preparing their lively three- and six-year-olds for the unusual treat of seeing a fellow human done to death.

The High Priest of Ptah generously decided to make it up with his rival, the High Priest of Sekhmet, since the sovereign had chosen to honour Ptah instead; and sent him a golden statue of the lion goddess, life-sized, which was placed in the Temple of Sekhmet early on execution day. The High Priest of Sekhmet viewed its coming morosely, because he had learnt to know his rival's gestures. Then he handed the charge of the Temple to his youngest priest, and went off to prepare himself for the ceremonies. Cefalu and Meluseth inquisitively watched him go. They were intrigued by the general bustle, and sat side by side discussing it with their paws almost touching. It was the closest Cefalu had ever got to Meluseth, and every inch of him, now leaner and more muscular than before, boasted of hope.

'Whatever may be going on,' said Meluseth finally, combing out her tail with a careful paw, 'you can be sure that they intend to honour Me.'

In some manner all his own Senusmet had learnt of Tahlevi's kindness to Reuben in the gaol. So he genially sought out Reuben, and invited him to attend Tahlevi's execution, in his train.

'A musician so honoured by my sovereign,' he said in his grating voice, his eyes more piercing than knife points, 'should be seen in public.'

'As he will be, Senusmet,' said the King's soft voice, 'for my Majesty requires his presence on my progress to the Temple of Ptah.' And to Reuben he added afterwards, since he had fallen into the habit of making wry confidences to his musician: 'The thought that Senusmet's mother, the most unpleasant old woman my Majesty ever met, has been deprived of eternal life, makes me feel sympathetic to this wretch Tahlevi. I had not looked forward to seeing her again, when my Majesty became Osiris.'

'My lord the King's Vizier dislikes your servant,' said Reuben sombrely.

'A man the King honours is always disliked by everyone, until he falls and may be trampled on. Do not fall, Reuben, do not fall,' said the King, and went to be prepared by his servants for his splendid coming forth in a gold and ebony litter, borne by his noble guards.

The palace was almost empty. Everyone who could was going to the execution, or to the Temple of Ptah, or to watch the King progress through the streets and prostrate themselves before the living Horus. Even a number of tribesmen had ventured in from the outer desert, with their camels, and were curiously regarded by the people as they forced their way through the crowds.

Anak's irritable pride had been hurt that he was not to be seen in the procession. Reuben had suggested riding him, but the King had looked obliquely, and told him to walk instead.

'You will join the guards round my litter,' he had said in his sweetest manner. 'It is an honour.' Reuben had bowed, and said nothing. The King narrowed his eyes, and laughed. 'Poor Reuben – escape is not so easy as you hoped, is it?' he mocked, not unkindly. 'And leave Benoni behind as well, since he cannot enter the Temple – he might easily be stolen in the great crowds there will be today.'

'My Sovereign is always thoughtful,' replied Reuben stiffly, and had taken Benoni down to Anak's stall, where they could both comfort each other for what they felt was a heavy and unmerited slight.

The day's events started to unroll with splendid pageantry. Tahlevi and Reuben, it may be assumed, were the only people not enjoying it. The sun god Re had chosen to shine with special brilliance, and above the palace a hawk hovered, showing, so the people said, that everything the King did was in accordance with the gods' desire. It was hard to tell which was more dramatic – the King's setting forth from his palace, or Tahlevi's exit from his prison, which both took place at the same hour. In everyone's opinion the Vizier's procession towards the place of execution came an unnoticed third.

Senusmet was fond of sarcastic gestures and had sent his own chariot to convey Tahlevi. The poor fat young man was placed in it shivering and sweating, his hands bound, while the crowd almost swooned with delight, or ate and drank incessantly to celebrate Tahlevi's approaching horrible end. It was a gay crowd, for there is nothing gayer than a crowd which feels very much alive, waiting for someone who will soon be very dead. Some lucky people had managed to station themselves where two roads met, near the Temple of Sekhmet. It was here Tahlevi's procession would cross that of the King's; where the King's litter would pause, for him to see the victim borne away to justice; and where the Vizier would make obeisance to his sovereign, before following in Tahlevi's wake to the place of execution. The crowds were more solemn here as though they already felt the presence of the coming god. Even the tribesmen had dismounted from their camels and prepared to prostrate themselves in the dust.

Reuben walked amongst the King's guards in the procession, thinking sombrely that he didn't yet understand the King. Was this black day of Tahlevi's execution to be the occasion of his own forced obeisance to the god Ptah? Because, when he refused, he would certainly follow Tahlevi to the stake. He was keeping his thoughts resolutely off poor Tahlevi himself, who was beyond his aid.

At this moment a guard walking by the King's litter turned and summoned Reuben. He stepped forward, and the King, who looked spectacularly regal with the symbol of royalty, the enamelled uraeus or cobra, shining above his forehead, leaned forward and said, above the tramp of feet:

'Reuben – when we reach the Temple the litter is entrusted to your care. You will remain outside with my guard, until the ceremonies are done. There must be no unfortunate refusal today.' Then as Reuben bowed in acknowledgement the King leaned back again, and the litter swayed on towards the place where two roads met.

In the Temple of Sekhmet it was very quiet. You could have heard a mouse move, but there were no mice, they were all running about outside searching for crumbs. Meluseth was lying on her stomach at the feet of the stone goddess, with a worried look. 'I do not much care for this new gold thing they have placed in my Temple,' she had just confided to Cefalu. 'It is uncanny somehow, not quite right. I shall not be able to sleep while it is here.'

'I will protect you from any gold thing in all the world,' said Cefalu dotingly. 'But I agree there is something about it which makes me feel we are being watched.'

At the other end of the Temple the young priest was almost in tears. It might be a great honour to be in charge, but he would so much sooner have been outside running with the crowd to see the great king pass. He thought of all the magic the wiser priests could do, and wished he could work some as well, to let him watch the processions. Often, it must be admitted, he had listened at doors and had heard things he ought not, and phrases he shouldn't know. Very daringly, considering he was all alone with the goddess in her Temple – for he didn't count Cefalu and Meluseth – he decided to try out his youthful powers.

'With my tremendous art,' he told himself, shivering slightly in his excitement and not really believing himself, 'I will bring the very spirit of the goddess to the Temple, where she will grant my prayer.'

He stood up to face the goddess, but something about her impassive face of stone made him hesitate, and instead he turned towards the new statue of gold, raised his hands to her, and began to speak the words he should not know.

After a moment the golden statue moved, one foot forward, very slowly and jerkily, and then the other, very slowly, after the manner of metal walking. The young priest fell to the ground in a faint. Cefalu and Meluseth squeezed themselves flat in terror. Some way beyond the shadowed sanctuary the great Temple entrance invitingly framed the brilliant, crowded day outside; and the golden goddess, with her impassive lion's head, walked clanging out of the Temple on her feet of gold.

The litter of the High Priest of Ptah was following the litter of the King. The High Priest himself should have been in his Temple, properly robed, and waiting for his sovereign to arrive. But he had waived this honour, conferring it instead on his possible successor, and had desired to travel humbly behind the King as a symbol, he said, that even the highest gods of the land counted themselves honoured by the Horus, the great High Priest.

The King had looked at him out of his remarkable eyes, and wondered shrewdly what was behind all this. Yet he had graciously granted the request, and so the representatives of Ptah and Sekhmet were carried side by side through the streets, since neither would grant precedence to the other. (In the hierarchy of Kemi's gods Sekhmet was known to be Ptah's wife, but the priests were far from married in their outlook.)

They were now almost at the place where two roads met, and the Temple of Sekhmet was in sight. Even the front of Tahlevi's procession could be seen, winding across the road ahead. The High Priest of Ptah glanced sideways at his rival, and squeezed his hands together in ecstasy. He had arranged a little surprise, and he was very much looking forward to the result. If all went well – and he thought it would, because he was a methodical man who planned with care – the new golden statue of the goddess Sekhmet would emerge from the Temple just as the King's procession halted. She would place herself, jerkily as becomes a statue, at its head, and when it proceeded again she would lead the way to the Temple of Ptah, thus pointing out to the King once and for all, in the clearest possible manner, that even the lion goddess herself recognized Ptah's superiority. Once she had entered the Temple she would naturally vanish, as became a highly supernatural goddess. No awkward questions would be asked, and it would have been made plain to everybody that Sekhmet conceded pride of place.

The High Priest almost burst out of his litter with excitement, as they reached the crucial point. How he looked forward to the final humiliation of his rival . . .

His eyes were on the Temple of Sekhmet. The procession had halted. In perfect timing Tahlevi's chariot was passing slowly in front of the King. Then, in equally perfect timing, the golden goddess stamped out of her Temple into the sunlight, clanging, and surveyed the crowd. A monumental gasp went up. Even the King slightly turned his regal head to stare.

'It has worked,' thought the High Priest of Ptah, giving his shocked rival a glittering look. How he congratulated himself! He had forgotten nothing.

Except that crowds can run . . .

The Temple of Ptah

For a few seconds everyone was still as the golden goddess herself. And then, as she took another clanging step forward, the crowd moved with one great movement as a swell sweeps over the surface of the sea. It was not the sort of movement that could be isolated and broken up, but a vast uncontrollable force. Those people who were nearest Sekhmet's Temple fled from her path so quickly that it was small compliment to the goddess. Their action spread contagiously, so that within a minute the huge packed crowd was fighting and struggling to escape from what they feared was some terrible visitation and coming punishment.

The King's procession, Tahlevi's procession and, out of sight round the corner, the Vizier's procession, disintegrated, spilled their component parts like matchsticks, and were swept away by vast numbers of terrified people, senseless as herds of cattle in stampede. Tahlevi's chariot was broken up piecemeal by the crowd's weight, and he himself was washed over the side like a minnow over a weir. Reuben was borne forward and found himself under the belly of a horrified camel. The King's guards were running as fast as they could, and miraculously still held the litter aloft, bucking and lurching in their hands. Deep in their frightened souls was a vague sense that only the possession of one god could save them from another. It was their strong instinct for personal survival, and no loyalty to the throne, which carried the King helter-skelter to sanctuary in the Temple of Ptah.

The camels, with Reuben underneath them, had been wedged by the crowd into a small corner between two walls. Here Reuben knelt in safety pressed up against two of their owners, and watched the screaming crowd surge past in headlong flight. Suddenly one of the tribesmen gave a guttural exclamation and pounced out into the crowd, returning a second later clutching a sweating bundle of humanity with its hands bound.

'Tahlevi!' cried Reuben joyfully. He didn't expect anyone to hear him in the roar and rush of movement, but the tribesman did. His knife was out and at Reuben's throat almost before Tahlevi could cry, 'Stop! This is a friend –' and to Reuben, as the knife was reluctantly lowered, 'These are my brothers –' and again to the fierce-looking tribesman, 'Use your knife to better purpose, Shima – on these cords.'

Afterwards Reuben could barely recall the next few minutes. There was a hasty murmured discussion between the brothers, and then Tahlevi, freed, was huddled into a dirty white robe, a piece of which he wrapped round his head like a hood. Reuben remembered Tahlevi saying, 'Shall we try to get away together?' and nodding, and being wrapped himself, by one of the others, into another voluminous sweaty garment, while Tahlevi took charge of the knife, saying grimly, 'Never again will I fall alive into the hands of those devils, this be my witness.' And then arm-in-arm they had launched themselves into the flood, and were being swept away, able only to move in one direction, towards the Temple of Ptah.

'We must keep clear of that, at least,' he heard Tahlevi saying in his ear; and nodded, his throat dry. At that moment the crowd gave another vast tumultuous heave, and those nearest the Temple outer court, which included Tahlevi and Reuben, were thrust forward by compelling force, and found themselves, willy-nilly, borne through it and inside the Temple, helpless as Tahlevi had been when the chariot was broken.

They were brought up short against a pillar, and stood there panting, hiding their faces as far as possible within their robes. They looked like two of the dirtiest wanderers ever seen in the city. The crowd was now surging past again outside, not trying to get in. Just as Reuben, having recovered his breath, said, 'Come!' to his companion, and started to move from the pillar, he saw it was too late. A group of priests was forming a guard about the entrance.

'Keep your face hidden!' hissed Tahlevi in Reuben's ear. 'We shall be here a long while – if we ever get out again.' He himself sank down on his haunches, and wrapped himself up close like a dirty parcel. 'At least,' Reuben heard him mutter, 'this is the last place they'll expect to find *me*.' A loud sniff told what Tahlevi thought of incense.

They were there a long while – a long, long while. The crowd's terror raged outside like an endless storm. Within, although it was thickly crowded, some order had been restored, and a form of truncated ceremony hastily put in motion by the bolder priests. Up at the far end of the vast, dim, and gloriously painted Temple, near what Reuben took to be Ptah's habitation, he could see the King's litter raised aloft, and the tips of ostrich-feather fans sway gently to and fro almost in rhythm with the priest's chant. He was glad to know the King must be unharmed.

The chant rose and fell for some time. People near the sanctuary prostrated themselves. Then they all rose, and the chant began again. So it went on, and on. At last it ceased, the offerings and prayers were done, and voices acclaimed the Son of Re in a great wailing shout.

The King's guards forced their way back through the thronged Temple till they were near the entrance. The clamour of the crowd outside had begun to diminish, and the obstructing priests moved aside.

'We must keep away from *them*,' muttered Tahlevi in Reuben's ear, indicating the guards, 'yet get ready to go – fast.'

'Yes, but they block our path,' hissed Reuben.

He turned his head, and saw to his horror that the litter bearers were carrying the King towards them, stopping now and then for the sovereign to receive petitions.

'They will never take him out yet in this,' muttered Tahlevi, despairing. 'And if all those people at the front up there are petitioners –'

It seemed that they were. The litter came to a halt not far off – near enough for Reuben and Tahlevi to have a good view of the King, as he bowed down from his leopard skins to hear the plaint of some poor old woman. He was very composed; if his experiences in the crowd that day had shaken him, he bore no sign of it.

'The light is dim in here,' thought Reuben, 'in spite of those torches. And the smoke and incense is a help – surely we shall escape his notice.' But he remembered all too well how clear the King's sight was, and what uncanny ability he had to notice things without appearing to. Sweat began to ooze into his already sweaty robe. He felt his one chance of escape starting to fade. *Surely* those astute and piercing eyes need not, amongst all these people, glance this way? A mad conviction took hold of Reuben that he must get his mind off the subject, or the King would read his thoughts, and look up ... He began to contemplate a gilded pillar opposite, which was shaped to represent a papyrus bud. How graceful its curve. ...

There was a shuffle of feet, and the litter moved on. Closer. The guards pressed back the people on either side of Tahlevi and Reuben, and neither had time to move away themselves before the space behind them was entirely filled. They were completely hemmed in, conspicuous in the front rank.

Tahlevi shot Reuben an agonized look, and lowered his head further like a bull. Beneath the robe his hand fiddled with the knife. The litter had stopped again, while a young woman stepped forward and bowed herself to the ground. Reuben heard a muttered exchange. Then the King's voice, a little weary now, but still clear, said: 'The King grants thy petition – go in peace,' and the woman bowed herself once more and slipped backwards into the crowd.

Reuben became hideously aware how odd their position was. Why were they in the front rank at all, if they didn't intend to petition the King? One of the guards – fortunately not one who had walked near Reuben that day – was bending over Tahlevi. He was telling him to step forward, the King would hear him. Tahlevi stared hopelessly at Reuben. He looked quite mad with fright, his eyeballs rolling in his head. Suddenly his jaw fell open, displaying all his teeth, and he began to drool like an idiot. Even in the extremity of despair Reuben appreciated the performance.

The King's voice put a question, and the guard replied, making an expressive gesture which illumined Tahlevi's state of madness. 'And this', thought Reuben desperately, 'is the end of it all. We can't both feign madness. This is where I crawl tamely back to captivity like a pet dog with a gold collar round my neck, and am never more allowed outside again.' In that second he hated the King.

'Are you mad, too?' The amused guard's voice sounded in his ear; a rough arm jerked him to his feet, and flung him towards the litter. The curious crowd pressed forward. There was no way back, nor to the side. The guard's hand was on the back of his neck, forcing him before the King. He had only to look up, and he would meet those compelling eyes.

It was a bitter moment. He stared at the ground which seemed to heave under his feet. If he had had Tahlevi's knife he might, in desperation, have thrust it into the King's side.

'What is your petition?' asked the King's voice, just above his head.

He could think of nothing to say. The pressure of the guard's thumb burned into the back of his neck.

'Your Majesty –' he mumbled, very low.

'Quickly!' urged the guard.

'You bewilder him,' said the voice above his head. 'Release him. You crowd us too close. Get the people back.'

Reuben was left alone by the litter. He dropped on his knees, trying to shield his face in the twist of robe.

'Look up,' said the weary voice.

'Your Majesty –' croaked Reuben again.

'Get to your feet, man, I cannot hear you. Look up.'

Reuben flung back his head, and in defiance faced the King. He knew himself filthy, covered with sweat and grime, the twist of robe shadowing his forehead. Was it good enough in the bad light? On the litter's other side stood Kenamut, not paying much attention to the scene; and when his eye fell on Reuben it didn't even pause, but wandered on over the crowd. He at least –

Reuben stared at the King as though the cobra above the royal forehead had turned him into stone.

'What is your petition?' asked the King's voice again, impersonally.

In all the huge, shadowy Temple, with its glow of flickering lights, its masses of people, its brooding grandeur and its clouds of smoke and incense, Reuben could see nothing but the King's face. His lips were dry as he stared into it. He saw the recognition enter the King's eyes, slowly at first, then surely, like water filling up a pool, and a faint smile curve his lips.

Reuben said desperately: 'My lord the King, your servant desires only one thing – to return to his country. To his wife. He would not leave here but for this, O Sovereign, my lord.'

The King's smile gently mocked him.

'What prevents a free man from leaving these Two Lands?' he asked, staring into Reuben's face. 'Is the sovereign a tyrant to his subjects? I think you would hide from my Majesty you are a slave. How can I give you freedom, if your master cannot spare you? It cannot suit the King, to grant this petition.'

'My lord, my master can spare me – if he would,' replied Reuben, troubled. He remembered the King's voice saying, 'Reuben, you have lightened all my care with your musician's skill.'

The King's face was impassive. His eyes glanced round him.

'Today in this upheaval is the one hope I have of escaping my enemies, O Sovereign, my lord,' whispered Reuben passionately. He felt he was drowning; and the King was now staring past him at the pillar, and downwards at Tahlevi, who was so frozen with fright that he had failed to cover up his face again. Just before the golden goddess had come clanging from Sekhmet's Temple the King had seen Tahlevi very close . . . and he had piercing sight.

Reuben shut his eyes. He felt that he would never again be rid of the smell of incense . . . or the heat. He made one last effort. 'Let me go, O Sovereign, my lord,' he whispered pleadingly, 'and I will remember your goodness all the days of my life before my God.'

Kenamut was moving round the litter towards them. He was coming to speak to the King. The King waved him back impatiently, and once more looked down at Reuben. He sighed. Very slowly he drew one of his rings from his right hand, and held it out.

'Go,' he said. 'The petition is granted. The King's ring is a sign your master frees you.'

Reuben took the ring, and bent his head to kiss the King's hand. As he did so he heard a faint whisper in his ear : 'And do not let your friend take Senusmet's father with him.'

Then the litter moved aside to the left, and Reuben found himself back by Tahlevi.

'You made great conversation with the god,' muttered Tahlevi indignantly. 'Are we granted beds of gold for life? My heart nearly split with your folly.' Reuben said nothing. Now that danger was over he realized Tahlevi could not know he had been in the palace as the King's slave.

Just once the Lord of the Two Lands glanced back, before his priests and attendants closed around him. Kenamut walked beside him. The King's eyes strayed over Reuben and Tahlevi as though he did not see them. He looked like a remote carved image of a king, but sad and frail, surrounded and weighed down by the symbols of his exalted office. Reuben knew he was being borne away into a great loneliness. If it hadn't been for Thamar, he would have gone back to slavery.

'He will be a great man,' he said unhappily to Tahlevi ; who replied, 'Too great – I would not care to be buried in a pyramid, not for all the eternity in the heavens. Think of the wicked robbers who go free! Now let us vanish, my friend, while there is still trouble in this city.'

Under the Wings of Horus

When Reuben and Tahlevi emerged into the street again, the crowd had thinned. Fear was still its prevailing emotion. People wandered here and there carelessly, too scared to remember what they should be doing, or where they should be. Everyone approached corners nervously, in case they came face to face with the golden goddess. Many people were flocking out of the city, hoping to escape her.

'The brutal Kenamut is still alive,' said Tahlevi thoughtfully, 'but I am not without hope that the Vizier and the High Priest of Sekhmet are flat as beaten meal. Which way shall we go?'

'I have to fetch my animals,' said Reuben. 'I came to Kemi with a cat, a camel, and my herd dog.'

'And where are they, these animals of yours?'

'One is in the Temple of Sekhmet, and two are in the palace.'

'It was always my honoured father's belief,' said Tahlevi philosophically, '– the gods comfort him, nimble and practical old tomb robber that he was – that all men are mad at heart. Your madness seems to clear the surface, friend.'

'I could not go without them, Tahlevi. But I would not hold you back.'

'No matter, no matter. Death comes to all, one day. I do not fear it when it comes cleanly, with a knife. Which way first?'

Reuben hesitated. Then: 'The Temple,' he said. 'Most people will avoid it, if they can.'

'One of your wits at least still functions,' murmured Tahlevi, as they plodded on. 'Which is a comfort to me.'

The streets near the Temple were completely empty, and the Temple itself appeared deserted. Tahlevi and Reuben slipped inside as inconspicuously as they could. It was all silence and lack of movement within. The stone goddess stared ahead of her unseeingly as she had always done, and as she would for four thousand years to come. Fat Tahlevi trod carelessly, making much noise.

'Hush,' said Reuben. 'You will alarm him.'

'He probably fled with everyone else,' whispered Tahlevi, now moving on tiptoe with a rumbling sound.

'That is what I am afraid of. Look well around these pillars. Cefalu!'

Not a paw, not a tail.

Then, behind the stone goddess, they found what looked like two flattened-out flags of fur, drenched with sweat, from which peered out four large terrified eyes. One of the flags rose shakily, gave a tremulous mew, and trotted forward to press itself against Reuben's legs.

'Oh my poor Cefalu,' said Reuben, picking him up, 'you have been very much alarmed.'

'In no way,' responded Cefalu, rubbing his head beneath Reuben's chin, 'but it has been a little hot in here today, so we were reposing ourselves in peace and quiet behind our statue.'

'Come on,' begged Tahlevi impatiently, 'if that's him, take him. This last wit of yours is shaky as the rest, I fear.'

As they left the Temple they heard a very small sad mew behind them, and Cefalu started struggling to get down.

'The other cat,' said Tahlevi, turning. 'I thought it was dead. It looks valuable. Shall we take it too?'

'I cannot, cannot stay in that Temple by myself,' Meluseth was shrilly addressing Cefalu. 'Is this your great, your lasting love for me, coward, faithless one, abandoner of the distressed?'

'The honour is all mine,' replied Cefalu, who had reached the ground, and now pressed his nose fiercely to Meluseth's in a fond embrace. 'I fear I was overcome by the pleasure of seeing my dear friend again.'

'We should not steal her,' said Reuben doubtfully.

'I always steal.' Tahlevi placidly picked up Meluseth and shoved her down inside his dirty robe. 'It is my art, just as music is yours. One cannot live without one's art.'

'One does not get impaled for music.'

'To my mind that is an open question, and not one which will be answered till we are outside this city. Pick up your cat, man, and let us reach the palace without delay.'

'This is not at all what I am accustomed to,' complained Meluseth's furry half-stifled voice to Cefalu. 'There are all sorts of things hopping about on this coarse man's chest, which may get in my fur. But no doubt you will make better arrangements later on, since I have bestowed on you the great honour of my distinguished company.'

Benoni and Anak had heard of the day's disaster through a grapevine of small beasts and birds. It had been enlarged in the telling, so both animals were amazed and overjoyed at their reunion with Cefalu and Reuben.

Tahlevi now took command and proved himself as nimble and practical as his father in arranging matters. Luckily the palace outbuildings were deserted, since everyone who could go was out collecting news.

'Your dog is far too noticeable,' he said decidedly to Reuben. 'We must wrap him up in this old reed mat lying in this corner, and you must take him with you.'

Soon Benoni was trussed like a carpet, only the very tip of his nose free to breathe.

'What is troubling you, my friend?' asked Tahlevi, as between them he and Reuben hoisted Benoni on to Anak.

'Water and food,' replied Reuben briefly.

'Now here is no trouble at all.' Tahlevi sat down upon the ground and puffed. 'I have worked everything out for us. My brethren were off towards the pyramids, and that is where we shall go. They will supply us with everything we need, because they are so good at finding it.'

'Tahlevi,' said Reuben, looking at his friend very straight, 'why have they gone towards the pyramids?'

'Reuben, how can you ask such a question? These great tombs are a most famous sight, besides being the eternal houses of our god-kings,' replied Tahlevi piously. 'It pleases my brethren to visit these splendours, like everyone else, and to meditate on what lies within. Now if you can get your cat back into your bosom, I will rebosom mine, and we will be off. You will have to slow your camel, because I am too fat for fast walking, but dirty as we are I do not think people will take us for anything but two wandering tribesmen. A pity', he added, fingering Anak's gold and scarlet harness which hung on the wall, 'that we must leave this behind us, but we cannot expect the gods to grant any man too much, all in one day; and I for one am content with what they have managed for us two already.'

In the cool of the evening the Horus, Lord of the Two Lands, was alone in his apartments. It was the hour when he had been specially pleased to have Reuben play for him, and now he refused the services of his other musicians and sat listening to the silence which, he said, was tonight better to his ears than any of their performances. An official of the royal harem had sent to tell him that a new and unusually pretty girl had arrived from Syria. The King signified he would see her the next day, or the next, and continued to sit alone listening to the silence which seemed to him, after so dead weary a day, to be alive with a disagreeable melancholy all its own.

'Why should I build myself a royal tomb?' he thought in his heavy sadness. 'Who could wish for this life to last for ever?'

One of his body servants, whom the King treated much as he had treated Reuben (the man had been his father's servant before him, and was proved discreet), entered soundlessly and prostrated himself by the door.

'Well, Hemi?' said the King. 'How is my Majesty's Vizier?'

'O my lord the King, that noble man is in great discomfort. An evil spirit torments his leg, which is, so the doctors have decided, in two halves,' replied the servant.

'Convey my royal condolences. I trust the evil spirit will depart. If I were an evil spirit, Hemi, and not a god, I should not remain longer in my servant Senusmet's leg than I could help.'

'Every word my Sovereign utters is true wisdom,' replied the servant with a discreet smile, remaining prostrate.

'What news of the robber Tahlevi? Has he been recaptured?'

'My lord the King, someone from the crowd, crushed beyond knowledge, his hands bound, has been shown to the Vizier's servants by the guards,' replied Hemi evasively.

'Very wise,' commented the King with a grim smile, 'else they would all be dead by dawn. And what else, Hemi?'

'Your Majesty will be shocked to learn that within the golden goddess Sekhmet there was a man. A young priest of Ptah.'

'It does not surprise me in the least. In fact, I expected it. This is just the sort of thing that would happen to cause general misery – even mine,' the King added beneath his breath.

'And to my Sovereign, my lord, the Vizier – kissing his sovereign's feet – sends this message: "Is it not the will of my Sovereign, my lord, that this man shall be publicly impaled so soon as the noble Vizier is recovered?"'

'Convey to my noble Vizier,' said the King slowly, 'that his sovereign always holds his wishes dear, but the man is already disposed of and as one dead.'

'It is done, my lord the King.'

'And convey to the man himself my most secret command that he shall leave my Kingdom instantly and not return.'

'My Sovereign's orders are obeyed.'

'Also, send to my Majesty's High Priest of Ptah my fatherly advice that he should do the same with all speed – before the Vizier's evil spirit can depart.'

'My Sovereign's orders are obeyed.'

'What – more, Hemi?' asked the King, as the servant remained.

'Your Majesty, it has come to the exalted Senusmet's ears that my lord the King's musician has not returned to the palace. That his animals are missing and two cats from the Temple of Sekhmet. Now is it not the will of my Sovereign, my lord, says the Vizier, that a careful search may be made for this felonious young man, that when caught he may be punished with all ferocity for so rewarding your Majesty's royal kindness by escape and theft?'

'Alas, my noble Vizier is greatly troubled by evil spirits today,' said the King thoughtfully, 'for he has been misinformed. True – it had reached my Majesty's ears that the animals are missing. In the hubbub there has been much theft abroad. When the golden goddess appeared the musician Reuben was flung beneath some camels, and it is feared he went the way of many others. The court will mourn the loss of genius.

'Remind my Vizier again of the royal pleasure in his

own survival and say: My Majesty trusts he will take no step in future which might impair his health; for I believe him wise enough to act so he may keep it in my service. Go and repeat these my very words, Hemi, and do not leave one out. I would be understood.'

'My Sovereign, my lord is as always instantly obeyed,' replied the trusted servant, smiling, and withdrew.

The Lord of the Two Lands was very tired. He lay on his couch looking at his hands, and wondering through what adventures his missing ring of carnelian and turquoise would pass, and if Reuben would find his wife again. Thoughts of the pretty girl from Syria came into his mind, and the silence seemed suddenly more friendly, and he slept.

Farewell, My Friend . . .

The pyramids were almost as white by night as by day. They burned with a malignant whiteness barely distinguishable from a white sky. They had a fierce beauty, fed by what lay around them: hundreds of thousands of men had toiled all day in the burning eye of the sun to raise them, and had been worn and thirsty; and many had died. Their bones lay beneath the desert. Great kings had laid them there: the bones of the labourers, white, and buried in a gold casing of sand; near the bones of the kings encased in gold, buried in a white casing of stone. And in the night the bones of the buried men and the bones of the kings held speech together.

'We are prisoners,' sighed the kings' bones, 'in a mountain of stone. It presses us down, rising between us and the stars. The priests have taken their lamps, and gone. They called us the sun, but it is dark in here, and we give no light. We have raised a mountain of stone – it has fallen on us, and the sun is outside.'

'We sing with the stars,' claimed the labourers' bones. 'Year by year we are sifted into golden sand, and fly back to the sun as dust on the wind. You set us free, O kings, when you enslaved us. What a jest, great sun-gods, buried deep in your mountains of stone! You cracked your whips about our sides, but they have stung your own. Poor kings who fooled yourselves – you will never see the sun again: we have laboured too well.'

The bones in the sand fell to chuckling, and a crack ran

all the way down a pyramid's limestone casing as though lightning had struck it. So it had – lightning of a king's grief. Yet not all his grief was strong enough to dislodge a single stone. A small desert bone gave a compassionate sob near Reuben's ear.

'I don't like this place at all,' said Cefalu, curling himself tight and small inside Reuben's robe. 'No respectable cat would be seen dead in it.'

At the night's darkest hour they heard something coming like a fast wind. 'Pursuit?' thought Reuben, cold with danger, and cocked an ear. A huddled shape shot past them riding at full speed, and vanished beyond their makeshift camp. It was the High Priest of Ptah, leaving as fast as he could to start a new life elsewhere.

When at dawn the pyramids became white flames with gilded tips Reuben woke Tahlevi, while the tribesmen slept on beside their camels.

'I do not think I shall come with you, after all,' said Tahlevi thoughtfully, his eyes on the pyramids, which seemed to exercise a fascination over him. 'I should surely drown up there, and, according to what you believe, they wouldn't have me on the Ark. Something tells me, anyway, that this flood of yours may not reach too far.'

For during the escape Reuben had told him all about Noah's prophecy, and what was due to happen, and how worried he himself felt about the King. He had described his life in the palace to Tahlevi too. Now he returned to the subject that bothered him most.

'I didn't tell the King,' he said, 'about the flood. Because what was the use? He would never have left his people. He is a good man – perhaps something will happen to prevent it.'

'I expect it will be local,' Tahlevi repeated, his eyes still on the pyramids. 'No one would want to destroy everything in Kemi, it is full of rich and lovely things, as well as some terrible scoundrels. And there is this good King, as you say.'

'O Tahlevi, please do not get yourself impaled,' begged Reuben, alarmed. He was sure he knew what was in his friend's mind.

'Not I,' said Tahlevi comfortably, feeling his knife beneath the robe.

'There are so many people near the pyramids,' insisted Reuben, 'priests in the mortuary temple, for instance; and others going up and down the causeway. Why, it's quite dangerous to be so close as we are now. Your brethren are horribly unwise – the King warned me not to let you take Senusmet's father!'

'Do not worry,' said Tahlevi, with a closed look. 'It's not the Vizier's father I am thinking of. If the flood should reach as far as here, and you in your Ark should see me bobbing about in it, I hope you will insist on having me dragged aboard. I could safely promise your old man Noah not to steal any more, because –' he added wistfully, 'there would be nothing left to steal, would there?'

Reuben laughed, and promised.

After Anak had been reloaded, Tahlevi accompanied them a little way, to show the direction they should go.

'Did my brethren', he pointed back towards the still sleeping tribesmen, 'give you all you need, last night?'

'Everything,' said Reuben gratefully. 'Almost all they had. They would take no refusal. I am for ever in their debt.'

'Do not worry – they will soon get more,' said Tahlevi cheerfully. 'I wish you well, my friend. Thank you for pleading to the King on my behalf – not many men would have recalled the small service I did you in prison. Have you that white cat safe? Ah yes – I see you have her near Benoni.' For Meluseth's anxious blue eyes and white whiskers were just visible high up on Anak's hump.

'Tahlevi, she is yours, really, but I take her willingly, because I know Cefalu will never forgive me if I don't. God protect you, my friend, and –' Reuben grinned – 'try to keep your artist's instincts under control. At least never take them near the Vizier or the High Priest of Sekhmet again.'

'Ah – that reminds me.' Fat Tahlevi looked down at the sand, and blushed slightly as Reuben was making Anak kneel so that he could mount. 'Before you go, would you do me the small service of searching me?' As Reuben stared, he continued quickly, 'You see, I've trained my hands so well that sometimes they act without my knowledge, just as you can hum a song without realizing it. And it's in my mind that they may have been busy since dawn, even against you, my friend.'

Reuben started to laugh. 'Tahlevi, I wouldn't like to do such a thing! I am sure you've taken nothing from me. I would have felt it.'

'No, you would not.' Tahlevi spoke with pride. 'My hands have a genius to match yours – do search me; see, we will do it together. And we shall find something, but I am not sure what –'

Together they carefully examined him, and turned his robe inside out. They found the King's ring, Reuben's pipe, and Cefalu.

'There,' said Tahlevi, laughing all over his good-natured face, 'do not doubt my artistry again, fellow genius. Go quickly, now. I fear I shall miss your company; but if you linger I will probably have Anak away from underneath you –'

He helped Reuben to mount, with the indignant Cefalu this time tucked away amongst his master's water bottles.

'Farewell, dear Tahlevi.' Reuben was much moved. 'And do be careful.'

'Of course I shall be careful. I am just going now to take

a small stroll towards the pyramids. The air is so fresh ...
Aie! How beautiful they are in the morning sun. It is in my
mind that on this North side I have spied a little crack,
which may lead to a concealed entrance, or may not –
Once more, fare you well. Be happy, my friend.'

'Farewell, Tahlevi. Be happy too,' said Reuben. 'But I
wish you would come as well.'

'I wish so too, in a way. Yet I fear my happiness depends
on a concealed North entrance. Perhaps we shall meet again
one day. Indeed, I feel it in my heart.'

Tahlevi stood there, his broad face beaming sorrowfully,
and waved them off into the desert. After a short distance
Reuben reined in Anak, and looked back. He could just
make out a rotund determined figure making its way towards the flame-white pyramids, with their tips of gold.

Lion!

'I am getting tired of this adventure,' said Cefalu, washing his nose with his paw. 'It has gone on too long.'

He was sitting on one of Reuben's knees, while Anak plod-plodded through the country far North-east of the Bitter Lakes.

As a matter of fact, they were all tired of it. And they were tired of Meluseth, too, who was sitting on Reuben's other knee, and had been boasting all day about her ancestry, her beauty, and her magical powers over men and animals. Benoni was cantering some way behind, to escape the sound of her plaintive continual mew. Even Cefalu's love was in that precarious state when he yearned to knock his beloved on the head to stop her annoying other people. He was also wondering if a plain black cat from someone's kitchen, uninteresting perhaps but domestic to the tip of her tail, might not have made him a better, quieter wife.

'– so that is what the High Priest said to me, he said,' Meluseth ended, triumphantly, 'and then we had a little festival, to praise Sekhmet for my courage.' She peered upwards at Reuben to see how he had taken it, and found him yawning. 'I am disappointed in your master,' she said sharply to Cefalu. 'He seems dull, almost dim-witted. I do not believe he has taken in one word I have been saying. I trust he will not try to lord it over me, because it is what I am not accustomed to.'

'Why should he?' asked Cefalu. 'He's not interested enough. He was high in the King's favour, you know,' he added with pride.

'That is what he says,' said Meluseth darkly.

'It is true, if he says so.'

Meluseth boxed at Cefalu's ear.

'Cats,' said Reuben desperately, as the paw misfired and hit his knee, 'stop quarrelling up here, or you can walk. Now let us talk of something else. Cefalu – do you realize we are going back to Thamar without our lions? We mustn't do that – it was part of my bargain with the Lord Ham. I have been keeping an eye out all the way, but not one have I seen. And if I did see it, I should doubt my ability to explain the situation to the mighty beast.'

'You need have no worries there,' put in Meluseth, 'I should take it upon myself to arrange matters for you all. How fortunate you are to have me with you.'

'A lion can be quite alarming,' said Reuben drily.

'Not to one who has had a lioness's Temple of her own. I should simply look at him, and that would be enough. It would be magic, you see.'

No one said anything, except that Anak gave a ribald cough. Meluseth sat dreaming about lions. She had only seen one carved in stone, and in real life she thought it would be quite small, a bit larger than Cefalu perhaps, but more handsome. As they rode along she wondered if this lion of her imagination would bear her off into the desert and declare himself. Now and then something irritated deep in her fur, the thought of Tahlevi's chest would intrude, and she would scratch.

Quite suddenly Benoni increased his speed, and came breathless alongside. 'I've seen a Shape,' he was panting, 'over there.'

Reuben halted Anak and slipped to the ground, holding the cats in his arms. There was a hillock of sand just alongside them, and beyond it was scrub, and then more desert. Some way off a piece of the sand seemed to be moving towards them.

Anak dilated his nostrils. 'Lion!' he said; and moved uneasily. Benoni quietly lay down upon the sand, while his eyes continued to observe. Cefalu held tight to Reuben's shoulder, but Meluseth fluffed out her fur and preened herself. She was thinking how they would all worship her, when they had watched her magic. She hadn't yet seen the lion, which came rapidly on.

'Now ...' Reuben was trying to guess the best way to make contact with this noble beast. 'I'll leave both you cats up on Anak –' he was deciding, when Meluseth said imperiously, 'Let me down. This is my affair, you will see,' and took a flying leap on to the hillock of sand. Reuben made an exclamation of dismay.

Once she reached the hillock top Meluseth did not bother to look around, she simply strolled straight forward, her plumed tail erect like a flag of peace. She wasn't really conscious of things beyond herself, all the time she saw herself as the others must now be seeing her, as someone beautiful, mysterious and brave, on whose magic they could all depend. The lion saw a small white object coming towards him, and quickened his pace.

On a flat bit of ground Meluseth sat down and arranged herself. She fluffed out her silk fur into a round ball, curled her tail to the left as a symbol that she was receiving, and straightened her front paws. Then she glanced round to make sure nothing was missed. She saw four horrified faces looking over the hillock top, Anak's higher than the others. She turned her face up to the sky, squinted a blue squint, thought about her magic, found herself suddenly in shadow, lowered her head again and –

The lion stood over her, looking down. Their noses would have touched, if he hadn't been so mighty a beast that he was far above her. She could never have imagined anything like him. He was a wonderful colour, better than the sand. His mane was tawny brown, and his large eyes, which were

golden with narrow slitted pupils, looked remote and un-
approachable. That he was a cannibal was plain at once,
for a bit of waterbuck was stuck to his front teeth. He made
a sound in his throat which was like the earth grumbling
before an earthquake. A rope of tail with a tremendous
tassel of matted fur upon its end whipped angrily from
side to side. He was far worse than the golden goddess –
and *she* had been going in the opposite direction . . .

Meluseth forgot all about magic, and about herself as
well. She thought she had died. She let out a piercing shriek
of, 'Save me!' and leapt backwards as though bitten by
a snake. The lion pounced casually (he was full of waterbuck; if he hadn't been she would have stood no chance),
but Meluseth by some miracle had dodged, and was streak-
ing back towards the others before he could spring again.
She went up Anak's front leg paw over paw, and disappeared inside an empty water bottle. Only the tip of her
tail stuck out, quivering as though struck by lightning.

The lion, much puzzled by her disappearance, slowed
his pace, and trotted thoughtfully on towards the hillock
of sand, behind which the others were now sheltering while
they made a quick plan before things could go too fast for
them. They heard the lion come up the other side, coughing.
Reuben was just saying in a troubled voice, 'Perhaps if you
and I spoke to him courteously, Benoni –' when Cefalu
showed himself for what he was.

As a matter of fact, it wasn't that he was braver than the
others. Really he had more trust in Benoni and Reuben than
in himself, but in spite of her tiresomeness he still loved
Meluseth, and he thought the lion was coming to dig her
out of the water bottle with his great paw. He ran lightly
up the hillock, and reached the top. The lion was some way
below him, which made their eyes meet.

'Peace be to you, O gracious lord,' said Cefalu.

The lion gave another cough, stopped, and licked the

waterbuck off his teeth. He regarded Cefalu with regal expressionless eyes. 'It was white, and ran, but is black and
stops,' he was saying to himself. 'And it smells better than
it did before: more like us.'

Like most people, he felt his own attributes were those
to measure by.

'O Sovereign, my lord,' said Cefalu, who had heard people
talk like this in Kemi, 'a great flood is coming. It will cover
all this wide land. We have been looking for you everywhere, that we may take you with us to our place of safety.
Will you honour us with your company?'

After that he stayed still, willing himself not to run, and
looking straight into the lion's eyes with as friendly a gaze
as possible – much as Reuben had looked at the young King
in the Temple of Ptah.

There was a long pause, which seemed endless to those
on the other side of the hillock. Cefalu and the lion were
communing with each other in silence, as animals do when
they are unsure about something.

At last: 'You smell of truth,' said the lion. 'Besides, something tells me – an inner voice, perhaps the spirit of the
great buck I have eaten – that you, though small, are one of
us. I perceive our nature to be the same. Tell me more.'

So Cefalu and the lion, whose name was Aryeh, held a
long conversation on the little hillock of sand, and in the
end sealed a pact of friendship, nose to nose. Aryeh was
then cautiously and with due ceremony introduced to
the others, and the six set off across the desert together.
There was no sound or movement from the water bottle,
where something very much ashamed was thinking things
out.

'Now we have Aryeh with us,' said Reuben to Anak, 'we
can lose all fear, should we meet a caravan coming down to
Kemi. They will give us a wide berth indeed.'

'You are right,' replied Anak, 'but I wish he wouldn't

trot just behind my heels. He breathes so heavily it makes me want to run very fast and never stop, like Meluseth.'

As they went Aryeh explained to Benoni that he was a solitary lion, since his two lionesses had fallen victims to a hunter. When he knew a lioness was needed for the Ark he thought deeply, and then said in his most majestic, magnetic tones: 'We shall be able to pick up a cub somewhere along our route, if we keep our noses open. But replace my own dear lionesses I cannot nor will not, just yet. A cub it must be, and very young, or I shall have to eat it.'

After a day's travel something small and flat crawled out of the water bottle, across Reuben's knee, and confidingly licked Cefalu's paw.

He made no sign, for he was very much ashamed of her.

'Cefalu,' said Reuben. 'Be nice.'

'This is all very well,' replied Cefalu, 'but I fear I cannot forgive myself for cumbering us with this fearless princess.'

'Thank you for saving my life,' said a small furry voice humbly. 'I feel I must tell you that I am not quite so magic as I thought I was.'

Cefalu sighed. 'That is all right,' he said severely. 'But do not put yourself forward nor talk so much in future, for you ran us all into great danger, which might have had a tragic end.'

And for the rest of the journey they had no more trouble with Meluseth.

It was on an evening many days later that they came at last to the country where Thamar and the animals were halted. And Reuben, shading his eyes with his hand, looked North-eastwards, and to his amazement and heart's pleasure saw Thamar coming towards them joyfully, a lion cub in her arms, and the elephants looming behind her like enormous bodyguards.

Ham Surpasses Himself –

It is easy to imagine how happy they all were at their reunion. Thamar was radiant; and if Reuben was less so, that was only because he hadn't yet told her about the flood, nor seen Ham fulfil his bargain. Also, he was still shadowed with worry for Tahlevi and the King. Thamar guessed there was a good deal he hadn't told her, but she was too thoughtful to press for explanations; and too content. The one thing she cared for was to have him back.

'Shall we stay here a little?' she asked later on, embracing him and Benoni and Cefalu all at the same time. 'It's so lovely to be away from everyone. Particularly that disgusting Ham. How did such good people as the Noahs have such a monstrous son?' Then she bit her lip. Too late.

'Has Ham been annoying you?' Reuben's face had gone set and pale. 'Is that why you came after me, when you were to stay where I told you?'

Thamar looked down. She knew Reuben's anger would be terrible, if she explained all about Ham's behaviour. He might even do something dreadful that would endanger himself.

'He said you were dead,' she whispered. 'He wanted me to be his wife. I was going to follow you all the way, but I didn't know which direction, from here.'

Reuben's face became yet grimmer. He'd been expecting treachery from Ham, but nothing quite like this. For a moment he thought things over, then: 'I should like to stay here, beloved,' he told her, 'but I think we should be moving on slowly towards the Ark –'

'Ark? What is an Ark?' asked Thamar, staring.

'Tomorrow I shall tell you all about it, when we have the tent up and the animals started. And Thamar – that lion cub you found – is it female?'

'Yes, it is.'

'Then that's one good thing, for Aryeh. Where is he – I've not seen him since we got here?'

'Putting the cub to bed in a thorn bush, I think.' Thamar began to laugh. 'He alarmed us all at first, you know, but he seems only interested in the cub. He took it over at once, gave it a good licking to make sure I hadn't harmed it in any way, spanked it when it complained, and has now kidnapped it entirely for his own. It will make him a very nice mate later on – better than that mindless ball of silk Cefalu brought back with him from her Temple! And Aryeh has promised me that if he eats anything at all tonight, it won't be one of *our* goats. Shall we go into the tent?'

She took him by the hand, and led him in. As he went Reuben glanced back across the land, which was soon to be plunged in darkness. His mind was still clouded with anxieties – some of them heavy as the real clouds now massing in the sky.

'I've come back just in time,' he thought, 'God be thanked.' And closed the tent behind him.

Travelling faster than Thamar on her lonely journey, and talking much of the way, they soon reached the place from which they had set out. When they neared their destination the sight of the Ark, rearing up out of the landscape, was no surprise to either of them. They could see its bulk, black and strange, while they were still some distance off. And it was then that Ham, who had been keeping careful watch as well as avoiding his parents' camp or any work, came to meet them. He didn't look at Thamar, but his black eyes glittered arrogantly, and with one finger he stroked at his little beard. Reuben noticed he was wearing anklets.

'Well? Have you got them?'

'Why – have I got what?' asked Reuben, as though puzzled, reining in Anak. (Thamar was mounted on the other dromedary.)

Ham's face darkened with fury. What would Noah say, if he hadn't fulfilled his task?

'Man – can you not keep a bargain? I suppose you were too much a coward to go down into Kemi, after all. Yes, you just skulked out of reach and waited for your wife, and –'

Ham's face was now almost plum red. He raised his fists in the air as though to throw them at Reuben. Just then Aryeh came up behind him and breathed down the back of his legs.

There was no water bottle big enough for Ham, or he would have been in it. As it was he made the longest long jump of that primitive but agile age.

'He is swift as any waterbuck,' growled Aryeh admiringly, 'but his smell is bad, and he jingles. Shall I eat him? I have not eaten for some while. The cub is old enough to tackle an arm, I think –' And he began to stalk Ham with great majesty and purpose.

'No, Aryeh, please!' Reuben hurried to slip off Anak and placed himself in the way. 'You must not eat this man, or we shall never get on board the Ark.'

'Must I not?' Aryeh half-closed his eyes.

'O Sovereign, my lord –' said Cefalu and Meluseth hastily together from Anak's hump.

'Please, Aryeh,' begged Reuben again, as everything hung in the balance.

'Oh, very well – at present.' Aryeh lay down and began biting a thorn from his paw. 'But tell it not to jingle too near me, or I might decide otherwise.'

'Now,' said Reuben to his quivering enemy, 'do you withdraw the term coward, my lord Ham?'

'I withdraw it,' snarled Ham, fingering a dagger, and then added in a more mollifying tone, 'If you have a sacred cat from Kemi you can hand it over, and I'll take it along to my father tonight. You've only one lion, I see. Where's the other?'

'It's just a cub,' put in Thamar.

Again Ham ignored her. 'I'll take it, too.'

'Aryeh will go with you then,' said Reuben pleasantly, 'since he won't be parted from it.'

Ham hesitated. 'We'll all go together,' he decided at last, 'and I can explain I met you on my way. Did you say you found a cat?'

'Yes, indeed,' Reuben still spoke very pleasantly. 'From the Temple of Sekhmet in Men-nofer.'

'Wish I *had* gone myself,' Ham's voice was sullen. 'They say the women down in Kemi – And it seems to have been easy enough. Hand the beast over and I'll carry her. It will look more convincing.'

They had some trouble getting Meluseth into his arms. 'Nice cat,' said Ham insincerely; but she eyed his beard with dark misgiving, and spat on it.

This last stage of the journey was no easy one. Reuben and Thamar found it hard to control their laughter, for Aryeh felt this was as good an opportunity as any to teach the young cub how to stalk, and he followed Ham on his stomach, now and then making a sudden pounce which caused Ham to leap high into the air. Meluseth complained for the first time since her disgrace.

'This man's chest is not so lively as that other's,' she said, 'but he is not a calm companion. I trust we shall reach our destination soon, or my health will be affected.'

A few drops of rain were already falling as they reached

the Ark. There had evidently been a sharp shower, earlier on, for the hull was reflected in pools and puddles of water. Thamar and Reuben sat their camels and stared in admiration, while Benoni looked at it and all the newly arrived animals near it a bit askance. He had preferred the select atmosphere of the Palace of White Walls. Cefalu at once leapt down from Reuben's knee to shadow Ham and Meluseth to Noah's tent. So it was that he overheard the treachery with his sharp black ears.

'You have done a fine job while I've been away in Kemi, O my father,' said Ham, entering and making the proper obeisance to his parents. (He had removed his anklets and hidden them in his robe.)

'My son,' said Noah, much moved to see Ham again, and thankful to find that the boy had it in him to be courteous after all. And to obey.

'My dear, dear son,' said his wife, with tears.

'Yes, indeed,' said Noah, 'we have succeeded well, I think. At one time we were short of wood, but still we have completed things on time – Shem and Japheth have worked well. And so have you, my son?' He tried to keep the query from his voice. He could see Meluseth – but where were the lions?

'Naturally I've done exactly what you asked, father – brought you a cat from Kemi. It was too dangerous to bring more than one, so we are taking Reuben's Cefalu.'

'Kemi!' said his mother, crying. 'I never thought you'd come back from that black, black land, my son.'

'In truth it is not too bad,' replied Ham grandly, 'if you're willing to show you are a man. And it has fine palaces and – and temples and tombs and things.'

'What do the women wear, in that terrible, idolatrous place?' asked his mother, her eyes glistening.

Ham said hastily, 'Oh – and father: there's a fairly large lion outside. I've left him with Reuben. And a cub as well.'

'A fairly large lion?' Noah gave him a searching look. He felt something didn't ring quite true. 'And Reuben? Have Reuben and Thamar come back?' In one way he was glad to know what had become of them, and in another he was not. He couldn't bear the thought of forbidding them the Ark.

'Yes – and I'm afraid you may have to speak with him, father. He's pretending to believe I promised them a passage in exchange for something or other. We all know he's devoted to Thamar, and of course he'd do anything for her – but he needn't', said Ham, looking very virtuous, 'lie about it.'

At this point Cefalu slipped unnoticed out of the tent, and ran as fast as his four paws would carry him, his tail stiff with indignation, till he reached Reuben's side.

'What is it, Cefalu? What has upset you?' asked Reuben, observing that stiff tail. He was dismounting. The rain had temporarily stopped, but Shem and Japheth were getting the animals on board. Some of them didn't like the gangplank. The snakes went up underneath it, they felt safer. Birds, of course, flew straight in. Reuben had already guessed that there couldn't be two of every animal on earth here, and his heart was glad. Surely it meant the flood might prove fairly local, as Tahlevi had suggested? Perhaps it was just a test for Noah and his sons, and all the local tribes.

'– he's lying!' Cefalu's tail switched to and fro like a miniature edition of Aryeh's.

'Who is?'

'The splendid Lord Ham.' Cefalu spat. 'He's in Noah's tent telling him how he fetched Meluseth and the lions all by himself.'

'That was just part of the bargain.' Reuben went to help Thamar down. 'And no more than I expected of him.'

'Was it also part of the bargain that he should accuse you to the old man's face of –' began Cefalu, but he was interrupted by the arrival of Noah himself, who had a grave preoccupied air.

'I am glad to see you back,' he said courteously to Thamar and Reuben, 'for your disappearance had worried us. What is this my son Ham tells me? That you are expecting passages on board the Ark? That you say he promised you them in exchange for some service you have done him? He swears you did him none, and he gave no such promise.'

– And Reuben Reaps the Reward

'Oh, is that the story?' Reuben was very still. 'I might have expected it of this fine second son of yours.' He was wishing he had taken Thamar down to Kemi with him, and stayed there. Perhaps she would have been safer in the palace of the King. Although not if Kenamut had seen her first –

'Then what is your story?' asked Noah sternly. But more doubts about his son were moving uneasily to and fro in the back of his mind, like small sad fish in a majestic ocean.

'That he made a bargain with me. That I have faithfully fulfilled my part, but he has not kept his.'

'What bargain, boy?'

Reuben was silent. Early on he had promised Ham that Noah should never hear the shoddy truth from his lips. He looked at Thamar, and hesitated. But he didn't have to consider the breaking of his word, for Noah, who knew his son too well, had already guessed the truth. It was too obvious. Reuben had been away. He was an animal tamer. Ham could never have brought back the resplendent Aryeh alone.

He had already guessed the truth, and it could make no difference. He put a hand heavily on Reuben's shoulder.

'I am sorry. Very sorry. Whatever bargain my son has made with you –' his voice faltered as he looked at Thamar – 'he never should have made. He must have known I could not keep it for him. There is only one reason I could allow anyone else on board the Ark.' His aged eyes were full of tears. He patted Reuben on the shoulder, could not look again at Thamar, and went back towards his tent stooping for the first time in his life.

Meluseth reappeared at Cefalu's side. 'What is going on?' she whispered, flirting her whiskers at a hyena.

'A bare nothing,' said Cefula glumly, 'except that we are all to drown. Since I shall not go without my master, nor will the others.'

Meluseth looked fearfully at the sky, and then at the Ark's protective bulk. After a moment: 'I will stay too,' she said. 'It will make up for the water bottle.'

'Can he mean we are really to be left?' Thamar, very white-faced, was holding Reuben's hand in a frightened way.

'No, we are not!' said Reuben suddenly in a ringing voice that caused a rhinoceros to collide nervously with a hippopotamus which looked just like the High Priest of Sekhmet in disguise. 'Do not believe I shall ever let you drown because Ham goes on his belly like a snake.' And he walked over to the elephants, and whispered in their rhubarb-leaf ears.

'Move them!' yelled Ham, waving his arms about.

'Please move them, Reuben,' begged Shem and Japheth.

'My boy, you must move them, this is most impious of you,' declaimed Noah through his beard.

'No, I will not move them,' said Reuben quietly but firmly, 'until Ham's promise is kept.'

'You have done a great service for me, and the Lord will certainly reward you, but –'

'He would not wish to reward me by drowning my wife,' said Reuben, still firmly. 'Or he would not be the Lord. That's reasonable, isn't it?'

The elephants stood side by side, shoulder to shoulder, rump to rump at the foot of the gangplank. No one and nothing could get up or down. Animals already on board were leaning over the side to look, and animals below were milling round in circles. Some of the more easily discouraged animals were just going away (like the Indignant Grunk, which no one has seen since). And it was raining heavily.

Noah – seeing it was useless to argue with Reuben – went desperately into his tent to seek some inner counsel. He couldn't bring himself to speak with Ham again, for the very sight of his sly second son hurt him too much. Even Ham himself was vaguely aware that he ought to please his father somehow, and he decided to manage this by dealing with the fresh situation all on his own in the grand manner. To his eyes the female elephant looked smaller and gentler than the other which had boxed his ears, and he was hoping she could be startled into moving away. He had already noticed that a small silver-grey bantam had laid some eggs during the last day or two, while she prepared for loading. Ham took up some of these eggs and cunningly approached the female elephant's off side.

'Would you like something very nice?' he lured her softly, and as she swung her trunk inquiringly towards him he thrust the eggs suddenly and hard up its spongy pink tip.

There is nothing an elephant likes less than this sort of minor shock.

'Look out, you blind fool!' shouted Reuben, but it was too late. The outraged elephant gave a shrill squeal, shifted her hindquarters round so rapidly Ham had no chance to escape her, and deliberately sat down. There was a scream, then silence.

'Have I turned pale?' asked Meluseth of Cefalu. 'I didn't like him at all, but I feel most peculiar.'

Alone in his tent poor Noah was wrapped about in a cloud of melancholy. Until suddenly it was pierced and lightened, a strange peace filled his heart, and the still small voice within spoke to him once again : 'My sad Noah, you are most troubled. But your troubles are no longer quite so insoluble as you believed them.'

'My trouble is continual, Lord. It is my second son.'

'But you have only two sons now, Noah,' said the voice very gently, 'and they are no trouble to you.'

'Something terrible and final has happened,' said Noah with a father's certainty. And he wept. Large, old man's tears.

'Console yourself, my poor Noah, my reliable servant. Ham may be more manageable where he is, than as he was before. The best shall be done about it that can be done. So dry your tears, and take your three sons and their three wives and go on board the Ark, for the rain is coming now in earnest. Hear its approach.'

Noah, who had not understood, raised his voice above the drumming of the rain. 'My daughter-in-law, she who was Ham's wife, died first of all.'

'Yes – so you will take Reuben and Thamar in their places, to fulfil Ham's bargain which he failed to keep. For the world needs courageous men, and Reuben's music is too good to be lost ; it will go on and on, to his children and his children's children. Comfort your wife, Noah, for they have taken away your unworthy son to bury him. And now hasten with her on board the Ark.'

The light faded, the still small voice died away. Noah went heavily across the sandy pools towards his first command, while Shem and Japheth and Reuben performed their hasty task.

Then Meluseth, Cefalu and Benoni, Anak and his mate, Aryeh and the cub, and all the remaining animals followed Thamar and Reuben up the gangplank, over the side and on board the Ark. (The Barbary ape was very nervous, like someone going through the customs, for it knew it was carrying more than two fleas.) Then at last the gangplank was pulled up, and Noah stood on deck looking at where his son had died.

'Would you mind very much,' he said to Reuben in a hoarse, unhappy voice, 'if I renamed you Ham?'

Reuben was about to say, 'Very much indeed,' when Thamar gently pinched the palm of his hand, so instead he murmured that he would be honoured; and Ham he has remained in all Noah's records until this day.

'But neither you nor anyone else will ever call me Ham, will you?' he asked Thamar anxiously later on; and she lovingly replied: 'No – never, never, *never* – it was just to comfort Noah, poor old man.'

By the evening of that same day the Ark was already afloat, clear of the ground. The rain had come down steadily like water falling over a cataract. Reuben and Thamar were in a small cabin high in the stern. They were lying on a pile of skins, and were staring out into the storm. Cefalu and Meluseth lay stretched out very much in their way across their legs. Benoni was flat on his back beside them, dreaming of hunting, of Ani's hut, of luscious titbits from the King's plate in the Palace of White Walls. Anak, who had tried to get into the tiny cabin too, and had been rejected though with kindness, was sharing with his mate in larger quarters, where he could complain to the elephants and giraffes about favouritism, and this silly cult of small animals which left out everyone of size and importance.

'Reuben,' Thamar was saying, 'you're sad. Don't be sad . . .'

'I was thinking of the Noahs,' admitted Reuben.

'But Reuben – dear, dear Reuben,' said Thamar, 'Ham would have been so very dreadful, later. Think what they've been spared. And now they have you instead, which will be so much nicer for them. Play something to me, that will make us both feel happier. And do look at the storm! The moon has completely disappeared . . .'

Reuben obediently took out his pipe, but soon lowered it from his lips again. He was thinking of rain on the palace in Kemi; and if Tahlevi, deep in some tomb or other, was hearing it patter above him at that very moment.

'And Reuben – stop worrying about the King and Tahlevi,' said Thamar, who was very sensitive to all his thoughts. 'I feel certain they will be all right. I know it. Here, inside. Perhaps when all this rain is over we'll one day go down to Kemi together and find them there.'

'Certainly if we can, we will, my heart,' said Reuben, which made her feel a little anxious, for she could never quite forget what he had told her about the High Priest of Sekhmet, Kenamut, the Vizier, and being a slave to however good and kind a king. But for the moment she said nothing more. Then at last Reuben really smiled at her, and began to play as she had never heard him play before, for she had not heard him down in Kemi; until suddenly he felt happier and put away his pipe, and placing his arms round Thamar went to sleep, with Meluseth and Cefalu rising up and down on their legs, up and down, in a gentle purring rhythm all their own.

The Ark was now riding out the storm on waves which were beginning to ripple across the land from West to East. Angels whirred through the night like rockets, and purple and orange stars wheeled overhead while thunder cracked beneath them. Flying fish had been picked up from the sea somewhere by a whirlwind, and dropped down in the rising flood water, and now flickered across the surface giving out blue-green phosphorescent sparks which attracted many white-winged birds streaming by above.

Old man Noah stood at the helm, his hair and beard blown like a flame around him, and stared out with his prophet's eyes across the waters. He already knew that one day he would send a dove to Ararat. Everyone on board, except the helmsman, was asleep, including Reuben and Thamar who, oddly enough, were both dreaming the same dream as they lay there in each other's arms: of how they were living down in Kemi with Tahlevi, in the palace of the King; and all of them laughing delightedly at the idea of any flood.

Rosemary Harris

Rosemary Harris is a Londoner, but spent her early years moving from place to place being slightly educated by a succession of governesses and different schools. Trained as a painter at the Chelsea School of Art, she later worked on picture restoring at the Courtauld Institute. She began writing very young, but only switched to it for a living when her first play nearly made the West End. 'My first stories were dictated when I was about four or five – the central figure was a greyhound called, oddly enough, Greyhound. He had endless adventures underground by the light of one naked light bulb suspended from a tunnel roof. After the stories were written down by someone else, the illustrations were painstakingly done by me – I can still recall the matchless realism of that light bulb with thick black strokes all round it to represent the light.'

Rosemary Harris's earliest books were for adults and included two thrillers; then in 1968 she published her first children's book, THE MOON IN THE CLOUD, which was awarded the Library Association's Carnegie Medal. Since then she has written for both adults and children, and has become well-known as a reteller of legends, illustrated by Errol Le Cain. 'Writing for children is more enjoyable, and I come back to it again and again because it gives more imaginative scope – children have a strong natural sense of theatre, and don't mind how much suspension of disbelief there is, provided the plot has a firm beginning, middle and end and is convincingly based on character; this is exactly like writing for the stage, my first love.

I like animals, music, photography, theatre, and seeing lots of people. Too long in London, I start hankering for the country, and too long there I start hankering for London – and all summer wherever I am, I hanker for the sea. I would like to have a garden again, I would like to ski, I would like seriously to study the guitar.

Some other Puffins

The Mouth of The Night

Iris Macfarlane

'Before this,' said the storyteller, 'there was a king and a queen and they had one son . . .' or maybe it was a farmer or a fisherman, but they would be certain to fall into fantastic adventures, for these stories are folktales translated from Gaelic, and that means richness, beauty and vivid imagination.

Here are tales of a prince who had to endure his shoes full of water until he could find blackberries in February, a boy apprenticed to a wizard, and the labours set on the son of the King of the City of Straw. Here also are the great giants, monsters, princesses and every variety of enchantment, told with the haunting and sometimes spine-chilling imagery of the Highlands and Hebridean Islands.

These are new translations of stories originally collected by J. F. Campbell more than 120 years ago.

The House of Wings

Betsy Byars

'Liar!' Sammy screamed. 'Dirty, stinking liar!'

His grandfather took a step and looked down at his feet.

'This morning,' he said, 'your mom and dad was talking about all the trouble they was going to have getting settled in Detroit . . . Well . . . it just came about naturally that you would be better off staying with me.'

Better off staying in this deserted old house with its porch sagging and the paint worn off and the yard all overgrown with weeds? Better off living with geese in the kitchen and an owl in the bathroom and this crazy old man?

Furious, Sammy ran. Followed by the old man, hearing his cries of 'Wait, boy,' Sammy ran and hid, hid and ran. Then something happened. The old man called softly for Sammy to come back, and somehow he knew his grandfather was calling him for something more important than their quarrel. And he was right.